Paul Simpson lives in East Sussex with his wife Liz, his mother Judy and their Jack Russell Terrier Dyfi. He has three sons Thomas, Charlie and George and two grandchildren Troy and Monty. Paul enjoys walking, cycling, painting and watching television. He also enjoys the odd pint of Harvey's beer!

For Troy and Monty

Paul Simpson

GROPE

The Diary Of Judge Jury

AUSTIN MACAULEY PUBLISHERS™

LONDON • CAMBRIDGE • NEW YORK • SHARJAH

A CIP catalogue record for this title is available from the British Library.

ISBN 9781528995726 (Paperback)
ISBN 9781528995733 (ePub e-book)

www.austinmacauley.com

First Published 2021
Austin Macauley Publishers Ltd
Level 37, Office 37.15, 1 Canada Square
Canary Wharf
London
E14 5AA

The Beginning of Days
I Remember

1st Day

New Year's Eve in the village hall, can't dance but tried, drank an extraordinary amount, late night, massive hangover.

Hello, my name is Judge Jury and I am a judge. I'm trying to pull myself together this morning, as I look at myself in the bathroom mirror, my trembling hand trying to shave my old and tired face.

I'm a compulsive potato eater and my favourite dish is bangers and mash – the sausages from our village butchers are the best – and I like to smother the whole plate with a huge jug of Bisto gravy, mustard, pepper, and I always have too much salt, but I like it, in fact I love it, perhaps too much, and I suppose one day, it will kill me.

My father was a judge and his father before him. The idea that our surname, Jury, might have had some influence on our families' professions, I thought might be true, but to be honest, I believe this to be more of a coincidence, unlike in the case of such names as Smith, Miller, Farmer, Thatcher and Shepherd for example.

I keep this diary with me at all times and do not know where I would be without it.

It is small so I keep it in my pocket during the day and make my entries with a pencil, not only at the end of the day, but as I go along, because otherwise I tend to forget things. I do not record every day, as some days are a blur, and not all days follow each other, they are simply days I remember.

You must bear with me if you think my notes a bit random, but my mind wanders and I wish for some reason to record my life – as I have always done since the age of seven – for future reflection, even though it might bore you to death.

When I can't be bothered making the journey home to my manor house in the country I stay at the Ritz; it's only £10,000 a night.

When I wake in the morning at home, I often take a swig of Scotch, which I keep on my bedside table. It works for me but I would not recommend it to everyone.

Then I always have to be careful walking down my stairs because, for some reason, I keep falling down them.

I then reach for the switch and kick-start my day by turning the kitchen lights on.

I am now 65 years old, but even though I don't look like I did when I was 17, I am still the same person as when I first started my legal studies, even though admittedly a little more rotund.

People tell me sometimes that I can't do this or that but I can, and quite often when I receive their advice, I do the complete opposite.

You might think of me as stubborn?

Or you may even form a worse opinion of me, but you will not have the opportunity to do so unless you read on.

2nd Day

I woke early this morning, as I usually do, and am now cooking breakfast for Mrs Jury.

Eggs, bacon, mushrooms and tomatoes and I've got the TV on and only wish the presenters would stop looking at me all the time.

I had to be at the crown court by eleven, so once she had eaten breakfast, she drove me to the station where I kissed her on the cheek and then ran for the train.

Today I had to listen to the pleas of a politician, a government minister even, who explained that he needed several houses and enormous fraudulently claimed expenses in order to carry out his work. I had some sympathy for him but the defence lawyer went on too long so I lost interest.

When it came to summing up, I could not make up my mind so before I addressed the jury to give my synopsis of the hearing, I tossed a coin, the outcome of which dictated that I put an emphasis on my sympathy towards the prosecution's case.

The jury found him guilty and I sentenced him to six months.

3rd Day

I had a good day in court today and believed my judgment on the case in hand was fair and the right one.

It was surrounded by mystery and intrigue, regarding a husband and wife and her lover: a love triangle, which had ended in the husband, in a fit of anger, killing the lover. The husband now sat in the dock accused of murder.

The defence lawyer argued that the husband had not intended to kill his wife's lover, but on learning of their affair – by means of a text left on his wife's mobile – had lost control of himself and confronted the said man in the street, attacking him and knocking him to the pavement where his head hit, with great force, a concrete litter bin.

The defence lawyer argued for a verdict of manslaughter, and after the appearance of several witnesses – who had all been shopping close by when the incident occurred and who all saw and could recall exactly what had happened – the prosecution then struggled to persuade the jury otherwise.

I had taken the French view, a triangular view, and intimated to the jury during my summing up that perhaps they should show some sympathy towards the husband, who was full of remorse and sat looking extremely anxious in the dock.

I concluded with four words: "A crime of passion."

The jury was only out for 48 minutes, and on their return to the courtroom, I asked the twelve if they had reached a verdict.

I asked if they had found the defendant guilty of murder.

"Not guilty," replied the head juror.

"Do you find the defendant guilty of manslaughter?" I asked.

"We do, my lord," he replied.

I now, bearing in mind the clear facts of the case, sentenced the husband to a year in prison and with good behaviour, he should be out in six months and all within the courtroom seemed satisfied with my judgment.

It is now the evening and I have taken off my dressing gown and am lying beside my wife, Beryl, in our huge four-poster bed.

She has gone to sleep so I'm taking the time to read some important legal documents regarding tomorrow's case, concerning a terrorist bomber's attempted conspiracy to commit murder in a London suburb.

Having received an anonymous tip-off, the police had made an early-morning raid on a terraced house in Luton and apprehended him, as well as finding enough high explosives to blow up at least ten terraced houses.

It seems to me an open-and-shut case and I believe I will be home for tea and shortbread fingers.

I've had enough for one day.

Time for sleep.

4th Day

I was right: the defence and prosecution barristers procrastinated for several hours, during which time I had drifted off and admit I did not pay much attention to their tangle of words.

I knew the jury had made up their minds from the beginning and I looked forward to imposing the strongest sentence on this man, the most severe sentence: life.

And when I opened my mouth in judgment that is what I pronounced: his entire life. He would never be released.

After leaving the Old Bailey, you'll never guess what, but because I'm a judge, and quite well known, people sometimes follow me along the streets of London.

I've got used to it and it does not bother me too much these days, but when it's that hideous reporter from the Daily Mail I quite often hit him over the head with my newspaper, the Evening Standard, a far superior rag.

It happened to me again today as I was getting into my taxi, and he definitely felt it and eventually left me in peace, rushing off, his camera swinging between his shoulders and clutching his crimson ears.

5th Day

I'm now cooking in the kitchen of my manor house. My cat brushes softly against my legs as I prepare bangers and mash with lots of Bisto gravy and tomato and mozzarella as a starter for supper.

When it's all on the plate, I put a large slice of butter on the mash and once melted, I cover it in gravy, a sprinkle of salt and pepper and take it on a tray and place it gently on Beryl's lap.

I'm sure she loves me, at least I hope so.

Beryl is sitting in our drawing room luxuriating, watching television and sipping champagne in front of a huge log fire and waiting for me to serve her supper on her tray and when she looks up into my eyes and smiles, I'm convinced she does, although I must admit, for some reason, for some inexplicable reason, I have my doubts.

I enjoy cooking; it helps me relax and gives me the opportunity to reflect on my week's work, which I believe I have undertaken in a firm but fair fashion and to the best of my professional ability.

I walked to the pantry but once there I couldn't remember what I had gone there for. And then I remembered:

Olive oil.

6th Day

For some reason, I woke at 4 am and can't get back to sleep. I worry, so I came downstairs hoping for birdsong, and make myself a cup of tea.

I might as well sip tea and worry as just do the worrying thing without the cup of tea while lying on my pillows.

Just to let you know, when possible I have four showers a day, and when that's not possible then one in the morning and one in the evening.

Just had another, creamed myself up and then looked in the mirror, accidentally of course.

I would like to let you know I looked absolutely fantastic, although a little tubby.

Then after a huge breakfast, Beryl and I made our customary way in my Bentley to our village church, Saint Michael's, to be bored to death by yet another uninspiring sermon.

7th Day

Today someone offered me a lift from the Old Bailey.

I suppose it was because I had forgotten to remove my wig and gown and probably looked a little out of place strolling down the Strand.

I snubbed my nose at him and said I would prefer to eat a piece of cake.

I don't need lifts from simple plebs.

I'd worked jolly hard all day and now I was going home to my manor and I would take a taxi like any normal person because I don't understand those buses, let alone those tubes and escalators.

8th Day

Facebook keeps asking me what's on my mind. To be honest, I find this very annoying because I'm trying to get on with my work, which is very important.

I'm going to try and keep off this social media website, which I tend to go to while munching on a sandwich during a recess, because I think it has begun to take over my life.

So I shut my laptop, push it far away from me on the table, pick up my legal papers and walk slowly back to the judge's chair for the afternoon session.

I was feeling exhausted and on my return to the manor, Mrs Jury was already in bed.

I put my head on my pillow and then reached over to cuddle her as she slept peacefully.

Being a judge involves long hours but tomorrow, and a mystery to me, my diary was free except for a breakfast meeting at the Savoy with a prosecution barrister who wished to whisper something in my ear.

9th Day

I had a call from this barrister, a colleague, yes, but with a slightly irritating manner, and he told me the time was 6.32 am precisely.

Jolly helpful of him, don't you think?

He wanted to remind me of our breakfast meeting at the Savoy. I told him in no uncertain terms, in a whisper so as not to disturb Beryl sleeping peacefully beside me, to stop being ridiculous and of course, I said, I hadn't forgotten. He had sounded anxious.

The trouble is, I've got my own Rolex and bedside alarm, and plenty of grandfather clocks about the manor, which, although their chimes are beautiful, remind me of time and how quickly it passes and however hard I try to drown them out with a pillow over my head, they always wake me at some point during the night.

So, I did not need an early-morning call from him, after all, he was only and always would be a short ambitious upstart.

However, I arose quietly from my bed and headed for the bathroom. I drove myself to the station and left Mrs Jury to sleep.

The Savoy, now newly refurbished at enormous expense, didn't look that different.

I walked through the hall and made a beeline, although early in the day, for the American Bar and managed to persuade the barman to mix me one of their fantastic martinis, which I threw down my neck before walking across the marble floor and into the River Restaurant where breakfast was being served.

I spotted the barrister sitting at a small round table in the corner beside the window, and as I sat down, I glanced through the window at the busy Thames with barges passing by, their wakes spreading across the entire width of the green river.

I decided on kippers while my colleague opted for scrambled eggs, bacon and tomatoes. I won't do that again as the kippers repeated on me for the rest of the day. We also drank lots of strong coffee accompanied by sweet biscuits.

Now what did he want, I wondered, sipping my coffee while glancing through the window once more, this time at the OXO Tower on the South Bank.

He asked me in a whisper, "Have you heard of the medina?"

"The what?" I said.

"It's in Marrakech, Morocco," he said.

"So what?" I said, becoming slightly irritated.

"It's just that," he said, shuffling awkwardly in his chair, "some of us, you know, legal chappies, think you should have a break, a holiday? We wonder whether you might have been overdoing it a bit, you know, working too hard?"

After our breakfast meeting, I strolled, slightly confused, up Regent Street and ended up in Hamleys playing with remote-controlled aeroplanes with excited children all crowded around me, jumping and shouting and trying to grab the little planes from the air.

In the end I lost my patience and, even though they were children, I eventually had to tell them all to fuck off.

They disappeared quickly, almost in a parade, out of the doors into Regent Street, where balloons were being sold by a balloon seller and tall red London buses dominated the street and black taxis passed by with yellow for-hire signs emblazoned on their roofs.

I decided I must go home but instead found myself wandering the streets of London until, finding myself peckish, I popped into Wiltons in Jermyn Street for lunch.

I sat at a small table in the corner and enjoyed a dozen oysters, beluga caviar and a bottle of excellent burgundy followed by beef Wellington washed down by a delicious bottle of claret.

After I left Wiltons, I walked slowly down Jermyn Street looking in shop windows and admiring the tailored suits, shirts and ties as well as the wondrous selection of cheeses on display in Paxton and Whitfield.

The afternoon was a bit of a blur really, the irritating barrister's words of advice constantly echoing in my head.

I hailed a taxi deciding to head for my suite in the Ritz.

But while in the taxi, I decided I could do more, after all we are only here once, no dress rehearsal, so I asked the driver to drop me off at Annabel's in Berkeley Square for an early-evening cocktail.

There I met a woman who seemed to like my portly circumference and my dancing.

We both ended up in my suite at the Ritz.

I felt I had betrayed Mrs Jury, but this woman enticed me into bed and I could not resist and she seemed to love my large girth.

After our lovemaking, I turned over and fell, exhausted, onto my soft pillows and into a deep sleep.

10ᵗʰ Day

Watching TV tonight in the drawing room, fire roaring, both Mrs Jury and I sipping champagne with caviar and creamed cheese on dried toast.

I was trying to chill out and forget about my work, and the barrister's suggestion of a holiday was becoming ever more attractive to me, so much so that I'd even been online exploring exotic places and had telephoned our local travel agent, asking him to send me some brochures on Morocco.

11ᵗʰ Day

I've had a day off today – some would like to call it working from home – and have just had another shower and creamed up again and I'm sitting in my pyjamas and dressing gown, smoking a cigar and sipping a large brandy in front of the roaring fire.

I've decided Mrs Jury and I must go away for a couple of weeks and I'm flicking through the holiday brochures on Morocco, which arrived in the post this morning.

I think I have decided on Marrakech, it looks such a lovely and interesting place.

A bit dangerous, I know, but I intend to come back alive to read some more legal documents and preside in the Old Bailey over even more of the most high-profile cases in the land.

12ᵗʰ Day

When I get to Marrakech, I intend to send you all, my friends, a post, updating you on our adventures here.

I think I've got over 10,000 friends on Facebook now, but I haven't got a clue as to who most of you are.

Sorry.

Mrs Jury and I spent most of the afternoon packing our little cases with wheels on, in preparation for our holiday.

We were leaving the following day. Rather sudden, I know, but with the splendid help of my early-morning barrister – who I consider a friend now – the legal establishment had moved hell and high water to alter my work schedule, with volunteers stepping in from all quarters to cover my court appearances. Jolly good of them.

We then prepared supper; my son and daughter, James and Fiona, were joining us.

During supper, I think James let this slip, he said, "You know what, Pap," that's what he calls me and I don't mind, "If you want more people to read your postings on Facebook, you've got to share everything."

My eyes lit up with the excitement of it all.

They left to go home about eleven, said thank you for dinner, and after hugs and kisses, wished us a good holiday in Marrakech.

13th Day

Just had the Sunday newspapers delivered and am luxuriating between clean sheets, reading and reclining against my soft pillows and waiting for Mrs Jury to bring me my full-English in bed.

The taxi arrives this afternoon to take us to the airport.

The taxi arrived late so I was incredibly irritated and shuffled about in the back of the cab, with Mrs Jury sitting next to me, all the way to Gatwick Airport, flipping through the Sunday Times Magazine.

The flight wasn't too bad although a bit choppy. The journey to our hotel from their airport, called something like Menarah, was bloody awful.

The roads out here, as far as I can see, consist of simply dust and large holes.

Looking forward to my shower at our supposedly luxurious hotel called Mont Gueliz.

I've just come out of the shower, which was not hot enough and everything about this hotel is dreadful. Mrs Jury agrees with me, and we are seriously thinking about flying back home tomorrow.

14th Day

When we awoke, we both agreed to give this ghastly place a last chance and decided to explore the medina, apparently one of the major landmarks of the city and our tourist brochure told us it was a World Heritage site and served as a commercial centre for Morocco with huge markets of local handmade leather accessories and, I must admit, beautiful fruit and vegetables.

But being an astute and perceptive judge – although it may have passed Mrs Jury by – I soon noticed gangs of boys having a great time pinching tourists' wallets in between the live music and kebab and pastry vendors who kept pestering us to eat at their so-called establishments. I wrapped my arms around my jacket to protect my wallet and told Mrs Jury to hang onto her handbag with both hands and clutch it to her chest.

The whole place was unbearably hot and dusty and I thought dangerous.

When Mrs Jury showed some interest in a leather bag, we really were in trouble. We decided not to purchase and started to walk away, only to be chased by this dirty smelly man, who could not have had a bath for a month, holding out the bag and offering it to us at ever-lower prices. We were apparently meant to barter but I simply told the filthy individual to fuck off.

I didn't want to be here and tugged at Mrs Jury's sleeve. We made a run from the market, looking for a taxi to take us back to our hotel as soon as possible.

After showering and a drink in the hotel bar, we felt relieved and a bit more relaxed.

We are both hungry so we have headed for the hotel restaurant and I suppose we will have to risk eating something.

15th Day

I don't want to describe any of this in detail but both Mrs Jury and I had a bloody awful night.

To say we were not very well is an understatement. Anyway it's early morning now, we had hardly slept, and were both still sweating profusely from what I presumed was food poisoning?

The dining room décor had been impressive but I now had my doubts concerning the quality of the Chilli Marrakech we both struggled through at dinner last night.

This dish was an aromatic tagine cooked with lean lamb mince with ginger, paprika, harissa and red peppers. At the time, I did wonder about the wrenching taste of the lamb.

We were now both struggling to get dressed and earlier we had booked a taxi to the airport.

We had decided to go home and I would not recommend this place to anyone.

The airport was packed with not only pleasant Europeans with colourful luggage, but also some rather unpleasant-looking locals.

We were flying EasyJet but the pilot didn't seem to know how to speak any English and the take-off was a new experience in aeronautic history and very frightening.

Mrs Jury reached for my hand several times and because of our gastronomic adventures the night before, we couldn't eat anything of course, but at the earliest opportunity, I demanded two double gin and tonics. Mrs Jury took hers with a quivering hand.

When the plane reached 35,000 feet, there was a terrible juddering noise and I asked the steward to explain what was happening.

He said he couldn't hear any noise and I told him to stop being so stupid and that I was a well-known and very successful judge and that I wanted to have a word with the pilot.

The plane was buffeting around a bit so my journey down the aisle to the cockpit, the steward holding my arm, was a bit precarious.

What worried me most when I entered the cabin were the expressions on the pilots' faces.

To say they looked worried was by any standards an understatement.

I demanded an explanation from the captain and also gave his co-pilot a stern stare.

By this time the plane was shuddering even more violently and there were several red lights coming on and noises coming from all around the cockpit. The captain tried to explain to me in a language I didn't understand, which was infuriating and he eventually shut up, thank goodness, when his co-pilot interrupted in English.

The co-pilot explained to me that the undercarriage had for some unknown reason lowered itself and this was causing the bad turbulence.

I told him, and I admit quite aggressively, that this was not bad turbulence but a bloody disaster and told them that I hoped they knew what they were doing because I was a judge and an expert at suing people.

I was asked politely to leave the cockpit and was guided back to my seat by the steward.

Mrs Jury looked at me in a concerned manner and once I'd sat down I explained the problem to her. She was quite naturally terrified and reached for my hand once more.

The pilot then came on the intercom to explain to the passengers the reason why the plane was shuddering so much but none of us could understand a word he was saying.

A buzzing noise then engulfed us, until finally what must have been the co-pilot saved the situation and explained the problem in a language we could all understand and said that we need not worry.

We were told that we would be making an unscheduled landing at Bordeaux.

Now, Mrs Jury and I happen to know the Dordogne region very well, having enjoyed many holidays in what I consider to be one of the most beautiful places in the world.

It's quiet, they have normal roads, fabulous food and wine of course and we have, over a period of many years, been invited to the château of one of my most successful clients near Saint Emilion.

I had a brainwave.

I would give my client and good friend, Gregoire Hutin, a call on the mobile from Bordeaux to see if we could come and stay.

And this is what I did from the airport lounge. What luck; he was shopping in the Saint Emilion market, and was going to prepare a gastronomic dream dinner for several paying guests the following evening and said we were welcome to come and stay for as long as we wished. He told me we were very lucky with the weather, which was really good although a little cold in the morning and evening.

I asked if four or five days would be pushing it and he replied not at all.

Mrs Jury was delighted and I immediately headed for the EasyJet desk to explain our new plans. Bordeaux's airport was very busy and so was the EasyJet desk, so I stood in the queue itching with excitement, whistling and relieved that our holiday break had been saved.

When it came to explaining that we intended to stay in the Dordogne for a few days, I didn't imagine that the EasyJet representatives, if they had any objections, would have a leg to stand on.

If they protested about my new plans, I decided that they would not know what had hit them. After all they had nearly killed us all, and I was certainly not going to spend more time than I had to in this Lego-style airport while they made efforts to fix the problem with the aeroplane.

Eventually my turn in the queue came and I was, at last, being addressed by a smartly dressed female EasyJet representative who, after I'd explained our intention to stay in

France, told me that my new holiday hopes would result in Mrs Jury and me losing our return tickets to Gatwick.

Well, you can imagine how that went down.

Like a lead balloon, rather like our injured plane.

I don't mind telling you I went bonkers.

As a judge, I am very used to handling confrontational situations and I thought I could handle this one.

After a few moments, my protestations resulted in several more staff being called to restrain me and they said that if I did not calm down they would remove my wife and me from the so-called airport and they would call the police.

After a while, I decided to stop struggling and take the alternative route and threaten them with court action, and not only that but a lot of bad publicity. The manager then arrived, looked at my passport, realised I was a judge, and a combination of this and my last words seemed to have done the trick.

Suddenly, they could not do enough for me and a taxi was arranged for me and Mrs Jury to Saint Emilion at no charge with a full refund of our plane tickets.

The taxi driver put our luggage in the boot and we were off.

I smiled at Mrs Jury and tapped her on the knee with delight as we made our way out of Bordeaux airport and onwards towards the vineyards.

Gregoire was standing on the steps leading up to the front door of his château waiting to greet us. The taxi swung across the drive, scattering the gravel, and came to a blinding halt, covered in dust.

Generally I like French taxi drivers but I was not at all keen on this one and was most certainly not going to tip him. He'd driven like a bloody lunatic so I got out as soon as I could, told Mrs Jury to do the same, and then, slamming the rear door as hard as I could, I retrieved our luggage from the boot of the Peugeot, refusing any assistance from Jean, the so-called taxi driver.

Just to let you know, Gregoire's château is fucking huge and dates from 1764. It was not a hotel but several of the rooms in this enormous building were used as short holiday lets, with the bonus of fine French cuisine, prepared by Gregoire and his kitchen crew, trips on canoes on the Dordogne and endless walking and cycling amongst the beautiful vines.

That night, after a quiet supper with Gregoire, we lay within clean sheets, surrounded by French tapestries.

He provided dinner three times a week at the château, allowing his guests to explore other gastronomic venues he recommended in the area. And tonight was one of those nights he did not usually cook, so we had a simple supper around the kitchen table, and after giving him a résumé of our travelling sagas, we caught up on old times.

The Aga kept us warm and we enjoyed an omelette, baguette and a carafe of claret. It was marvellous to see him again.

I could tell Mrs Jury was happy and content, and, as my arm went to rest on her shoulder, when reaching for the carafe, I could tell my luck was in tonight, for a change.

After my exhausting exertions with Mrs Jury, I slept well and without interruption and had a good night.

16th Day

It's all about me, and yes it has always been about me, and that is why I am sitting in the most important place, at the head of this huge French table with Gregoire and his paying guests listening to my every word.

The dining room is laid out in true Louis XVI style.

A slightly strange thought entered my head. I only wished I could have been dressed in my wig and gown.

I was so interesting that wonderful evening. The table was covered in candles and Napoleonic silver and cut glass and the walls covered with paintings of French kings and several of Marie Antoinette, the French Revolution, and a small oil painting of a young Napoleon Bonaparte hung beside the door to the kitchen.

A lady to my left asked me if we had enjoyed our trip to Marrakech. I controlled my ever-increasing blood pressure and said no we certainly did not.

I touched my lips with my napkin and said she looked very pretty and warned her, if she had any sense, never to set foot in the place.

I added, not intending to be rude, that if she wished to stay in a good state of health and not be robbed rotten it would be in her interest not to venture there. Other than that I was not prepared to talk about it.

All the guests enjoyed my very amusing conversation and I had a wonderful evening and I'm sure everyone else at the table did too.

I dominated the conversation brilliantly and when it was time for bed, one of Gregoire's servants guided Mrs Jury and I up endless stairs and corridors and eventually, exhausted, we were let into our bedroom.

I collapsed onto the bed, admittedly a little worse for wear from the delicious local claret.

Mrs Jury fell into bed immediately beside me with all her clothes on while I at least removed my trousers but while attempting to remove my socks fell luckily into bed and passed out before I knew it.

17th Day

Today, after eating croissants for breakfast – they're so boring and dry and always stick to the top of my mouth – everyone insisted on hiring those French scooter things from Gregoire, who had a barn full of them, and then we all headed for the hills but I wasn't very keen. Mainly because I had a dreadful hangover. But even so I decided to go along with it anyway. Foolishly I did not stick to my guns and refuse to go.

So we set forth, in one chaotic uncontrollable rush, like the start of some grand prix, our rear wheels spraying gravel all over the lawn in front of the château.

To begin with my bloody scooter took several kicks to start so I immediately didn't like the thing.

We eventually arrived – after gliding up the hills, making use of every inch of the roads, and taking care because of the morning dampness – at a fantastic restaurant with marvellous views over the valley called Le Clos Saint Font, which played Harry Belafonte, apparently all the time.

On our way back to Gregoire's château, for fun we weaved our way through the narrow grass tracks that made their way north, south, east and west like the streets and avenues of New York between the vineyards. I must admit this was wonderful, but when I fell off because I skidded on some gravel and loose earth, which was not my fault of course, my friends took me to the local hospital in Sainte-Foy-la-Grande.

French hospitals aren't that bad, and although the doctor ascertained that I had badly sprained my ankle, at least it was not broken. But swollen, yes. It looked the size of a melon.

Within no time at all they had my ankle strapped up tightly and had patched up my other wounds with Germolene, plasters and more bandages. The nurses then let me go, along with some crutches.

Gregoire, who had arrived earlier looking very concerned, kindly took me and Mrs Jury, who had been at my bedside all along, home in his Peugeot.

Thank goodness I was wearing a helmet.

18th Day

We took it easy today because of my sprained ankle. I now had huge bruises in various places and aches all over.

Mrs Jury and I stayed at Gregoire's château in bed reading most of the day. I was proud of her; she was really sympathetic towards me and was doing her best to satisfy my every need.

We were quite happy, and apart from my aches and pains I enjoyed the peace of our room and not having to converse with the other guests, which even for me was becoming exhausting.

Gregoire brought lunch to us on trays: mussels and pommes frites and an excellent bottle of cold burgundy.

I took my laptop out of my small roll-along case, and logged into Facebook and just got tapping.

Anyone missing me yet? I've got lots to tell you but I've gone into a slightly secretive mode, don't know why, wish me good luck and good night X.

And with that I lifted my swollen ankle onto the bed, lay back feeling pleased with myself and closed my eyes for a cat nap before I showered, sitting on my bottom with my bandaged leg sticking out of the semi-closed shower door. I then towelled myself, creamed myself up and got dressed for yet another dinner party.

New guests had arrived today at the château and Gregoire said he was looking forward to more of my scintillating conversation. I intended to go on all night about our excursions on our scooters and my accident. Then I would tell stories of some of my most famous court cases.

I suppose I'm a bit smug, but why shouldn't I be? I'm a very successful judge with very interesting things to say. It's as simple as that.

19th Day

I woke up this morning feeling bloody pissed off; I hadn't slept well because of my throbbing foot and me and Mrs Jury had had a minor contretemps before we went to bed last night, because I thought she was flirting too much with some French chappy at dinner.

I was feeling a little groggy, and when I reached for the glass of Evian beside my bed I threw it down my neck, only to find that it was my glass of Chardonnay from the night before.

It tasted good and gave me a flavour for the day ahead.

I felt in a better mood already.

Mrs Jury stirred beside me and I said to her that I was lucky to have her as my wife, even though she might not think so.

I then headed for the bathroom, limping and leaning on my crutches.

This bandage made my ankle feel itchy and was a bloody nuisance and so this time I took the bloody thing off and gingerly stepped into the shower.

20th Day

It was now the last day of our absolutely fantastic holiday in the Dordogne and although I had not slept that well again because of my swollen ankle, I was feeling refreshed and invigorated by the anticipation of my busy court life back home.

I could be nasty when I wanted to be and this was necessary, I felt, to be a hugely successful judge.

I'll let you into a secret though: when I go to my doctor he always asks me how much I drink. I always lie of course, how anyone can survive on 14 units a week? I've done that by breakfast.

Gregoire drove us to Bordeaux airport for our afternoon flight back to London Gatwick and in my mind said his goodbyes a little too quickly.

I just had this funny feeling he was pleased to see the back of us.

Being perceptive is not always a blessing.

21st Day

Back in Old Blighty now, and I woke up this morning pleased to be home and feeling a bit horny but Mrs Jury was having none of it.

I helped myself to a glass of Scotch to help me feel better.

I eventually gave up my amorous manoeuvres and as we were entertaining some guests from our parish for lunch tomorrow I threw back the bed sheets, which I told Mrs Jury needed to go to the dry cleaners, showered, creamed up, dressed and then hobbled down the stairs and set off for Tesco in the Bentley.

I think this holiday caper really suits me, I'm really enjoying myself. And my ankle is still feeling tender but much better.

22nd Day

One of my many qualities, as you know, is being perceptive.

One of the lady guests who was sitting next to me at our lunch, our church warden, was eyeing me up so I had to explain to her privately that I was a married man, not only that, but a respectable and well-known judge as she well knew.

While Mrs Jury was holding court at the head of the table and explaining to shrieks of laughter from our guests about our holiday exploits the church warden still persisted to the extent of touching my knee, so I eventually had to tell her in a whisper, below the loud discussions taking place around the table, to cool it!

Outside our dining room window, there was the sound of a frantic chainsaw.

My gardener, what's-his-name, saved the embarrassing situation taking place between myself and the church warden by interrupting our conversation when he called me on my mobile, which I retrieved from my jacket pocket.

He told me he was cutting down some trees in my garden where my potatoes live. I told him I knew because I could hear the bloody racket but not to worry and carry on and that I would come and inspect his work later.

As a judge, I am paid a lot of money but I think I am worth every penny. I am very good at what I do and you always get what you pay for and an added bonus is I look splendid in my wig and gown.

Now, when I get in a bad mood I make sure everyone knows it, as our church warden had discovered. You might wonder why I have just said that, but it is simply to emphasise a point, which is that in this life you have not only got to be good, no, sorry, *excellent* at what you do, but without doubt it also helps to be a bully.

The lunch had been a long and exhausting one so Mrs Jury went to bed early, probably to escape my advances, and I was now eating mounds and mounds of smoked salmon on a tray with some pepper and lemon juice and I decided to stay in my study all evening working on important documents.

When it came time to limp up the stairs to bed I was not entirely sure but I thought I felt a little queasy. My suspicions were focused on the smoked salmon, which was on offer from Tesco and I had thought tasted a bit funny.

23rd Day

I'm trying to look after myself, you see, but a night of being profusely ill from the salmon – and this involved quite a lot of vomiting – left me looking not only pale in the morning but my vision was also a bit blurry.

I stayed in bed all day with Mrs Jury waiting on me hand and foot. I think she really does love me after all and that French chappy who she flirted with at Gregoire's meant nothing. I hoped so.

I wanted to be fully recovered as we were attending a banquet at the Guildhall tomorrow evening.

24th Day

Anyway, you'll never guess what happened tonight at the banquet being held at the Guildhall for the Lord Mayor of London's convenience.

Anyway this is what happened.

And to me who sat in judgment on scum.

It just shows you.

Mrs Jury and I sat at a very large Georgian mahogany dining table covered in silver cutlery and cut glass and surrounded by a host of very important and highly respected members of our elite and high society, mostly businessmen, important civil servants and politicians. Either side of us were similar long and equally exquisitely dressed tables as well as more important people.

It was a wonderful spread and I suppose, once again, I helped myself to too much claret.

Before I knew it, over pudding, I groped the breast of a very pretty divorced woman sitting next to me. We had got on immediately and I had found her charming.

To be honest I don't know what on earth made me do it. I cannot understand what I was thinking about.

Anyway the conversation at the table, and indeed the entire hall, immediately stopped and the host of the party, the Chancellor of the Exchequer, asked me to leave immediately.

Of course Mrs Jury was flabbergasted and the doors to the Guildhall were opened wide for our departure.

I felt very ashamed and we never said a word to each other as Mrs Jury drove me home in the Bentley.

25th Day

I had a telephone call this morning from a colleague of mine, a barrister who I know very well, telling me this woman from the night before wanted to sue me.

I'm meant to do the suing so when I put the phone down I went into a bit of a flap.

I do drink, I know, so this helps.

After this conversation I immediately ran for the drinks cabinet, limping furiously.

By anyone's standards I think it is fair to say I got plastered and had to sleep it off during the afternoon.

When I eventually awoke I had the most horrific hangover and tried to compose myself and think about what I was going to do now.

I considered my options and came to the only conclusion there was. I did not have any.

To be blunt about this, I was in the shit.

Later that morning Mrs Jury discovered me in our bedroom, just in my underpants, cowering in the corner.

She told me to get a grip of myself and sort my life out.

Thanks, I said, clutching the velvet curtains before reaching for my trousers.

26th Day

Mrs Jury was not talking to me of course and not cooking me any meals and I felt my life had been turned upside down.

What on earth had made me do that grope? I felt better with myself when I decided to blame it on the claret.

I put on my wig and gown that were hanging in the hall and paced about a bit while limping, trying to make myself feel better.

But I was in shock I suppose, and really none of this seemed to help me come to terms with my dilemma.

Then there was a knock on my front door and two police officers were standing there. They said I smelt like I had been drinking.

I said I had been, but it was my own house and that if I wanted to do so, I could. I knew the law. I am a judge after all and it was none of their business. Not a good start.

Then they quizzed me about the evening at the Guildhall, explaining that the lady who had sat next to me had made a complaint of assault, which they were taking seriously.

"Assault!" I said. "You must be kidding, don't be so bloody ridiculous!"

After I had answered a few more of their questions they cautioned me and then walked me rather roughly towards their car, which had blue flashing lights on the top.

They seemed to have no sympathy for me and my ankle.

I hate smug people but I suppose I've been a bit smug myself for too long and now I've been caught out.

Things that go around come around came to mind, but you must not feel sorry for me.

I know it's all my own fault but what's going to happen to me now? I cannot bear to think of it.

I will surely lose my wig and gown and possibly go to prison.

To be honest I'm terrified.

My reputation and career are certainly in tatters.

At least Beryl gave me a half-hearted wave goodbye as we sped up my driveway.

When we got to the police station I was shuffled, again rather roughly, into an interrogation room and they told me to sit down.

They left me on my own, closing the door behind them. I felt drained and exhausted.

When the officers returned they sat down opposite me and began firing questions.

They asked me why I had behaved in such a disgusting manner.

I replied that I didn't really know what I was doing and added, perhaps foolishly, that I didn't think they really knew what they were doing either and did they know who they were talking to and that I would like them to bugger off.

These comments didn't go down too well and I was led swiftly to a cell.

27th Day

My recollection of the time since I was charged is a bit hazy only to say my claret cellar is missing several bottles and Mrs Jury has done her best to avoid me, disappearing for days at a time, from the manor.

But today's the day and I am now in court, sitting in the dock with this so-called colleague of mine towering over me, eager to ask me awkward questions.

I am in any other ordinary circumstances sitting in the judge's seat, observing the courtroom before me and the quivering accused sitting in the box to my left. Roles have been reversed and I am trying to retain my dignity and composure.

"You've been accused of groping a young lady's breast. What have you got to say about this?" the bloody chap who is supposed to be my friend, asks me.

I let slip that I could not see what was wrong with it anyway. I say everyone is doing it nowadays.

The court goes into silence and the judge calls for a recess and the jury are asked to come back tomorrow.

I think I'm in a bit of a pickle now. I must stop digging because the hole I'm in seems to be getting deeper and deeper. I think I'll try and keep my mouth closed, or at least think carefully before I open it once again.

28th Day

I was escorted by two burly policemen, limping to my new place in the world.

The dock.

The courtroom was packed and brightly lit and I admit I was feeling slightly, if not extremely, nervous.

My case had attracted quite a lot of attention from the press and there were all the usual artists there scratching nasty coloured pictures of me. The courtroom scene in which I was the centre of attention was familiar, but from a slightly different and uncomfortable angle. They are not allowed to take pictures within the courtroom of course but I'm sure the paparazzi and their flashing cameras were waiting eagerly outside, as well as newsrooms up and down the land searching out archive footage of me.

To be honest I was getting a bit of a buzz from all of this attention and I quite liked it in a way and I was looking forward to seeing their works of art on the television news tonight and in the papers tomorrow.

To be famous, oh my God, to be famous, the X-Factor veil I think had been cast over me.

My appearance in court was brief. The witnesses, the guests at the Guildhall – and there were plenty of them – all had their say while looking at me in disgust.

I ignored their disapproving glares and turned my head to my best side for the artists who were all furiously scribbling away.

I was sentenced to three months for assault and was to spend my time at Her Majesty's Pleasure at an establishment called Blantyre House, near Goudhurst, in Kent.

Apparently, you have to be good to go there. Because I used to be – yes, used to be, a judge, I had been struck off, of course, but I hoped to be out in six weeks, fingers crossed!

29th Day

This is my first day in prison and I am sharing a cell with a chap called Bogie; I think that must be his nickname.

I, of course, knew of Blantyre House because I had sent many guilty people to the much less inviting establishments and knew that Blantyre was designed to prepare men for their eventual release.

It's a bit like a boarding school really, and is an adult male category 'C/D' resettlement prison.

The buildings themselves are located in a country house, which was, I have recently learnt, taken over by the Prison Commission in 1954 and I am finding them surprisingly comfortable.

Within the first six months it is compulsory for the inmates to build upon their education, which will include obtaining basic skills, qualifications and taking part in courses such as healthy lifestyles, social and life skills, independent living and eventual preparation for work.

There are also a number of vocational courses on offer including IT, dry-lining and plastering.

I decided to try my hand at plastering, which was a mistake because, unlike my barrister days, I just could not make it stick.

But if you behaved properly the prison would allow you out into the Kent countryside to do community work, escorted by a prison officer to begin with and if you proved to be reliable and they didn't think you were going to run away then you were given the opportunity of gazing at the nearest one could get to freedom between the Kent hops and the pub on the horizon.

I think I've painted myself into a not totally unpleasant corner of the Garden of England.

Only wished I could sip a glass of whiskey.

30th Day

What's keeping me sane in here is being able to continue my diary and post my thoughts on Facebook to my many friends.

Bogie is a little annoying and keeps farting all the time and the smell he makes reminds me of a good curry.

My ankle was feeling much more comfortable but my wish was to be able to turn back time and not to have groped that innocent woman's breast at dinner.

I knew my sexual conduct fell well short of that expected of a judge but I was simply going to have to lump it and get used to these four walls.

To be honest I think a few of my friends and colleagues had become concerned about me recently, and my increasingly irrational behaviour, so to many of them this palaver had not come as a complete surprise.

But to my astonishment the food in here is jolly good and reminds me of the menu in the Ritz.

I reckoned from my experience, as a once successful judge, with good and not inappropriate behaviour, I could be out of here not in six weeks but hopefully in four.

But what's worrying me most at the moment is that I had forgotten to fill in my tax return.

31st Day

My plastering lessons are not going very well. The teacher is very patient with me and I listen intently to his every word and watch with interest his demonstrations as to how this plastering lark should be done professionally.

Mrs Jury is visiting me tomorrow and to be honest I'm a little nervous about this.

She has, of course, still not forgiven me and I'm wondering why she is coming, but it's probably because she simply loves me.

32nd Day

There are a lot of bats that fly around this prison. They are fascinating creatures so I suppose there is no harm in an older, larger version coming to see me today.

She won't be bringing me any legal documents as the press have had, and are still having, a field day with my exploits and I have been dragged by them through the mud backwards and, of course, I have been struck off.

When she arrived she told me she wanted a divorce.

I had been sued for a lot of money and I knew I may well have to sell the manor and she now told me there was someone else in her life and in fact she has been seeing him for some time.

Can things get worse?

Yes, well, probably.

I wondered whether it might be that French chappy she was flirting with at Gregoire's dinner party in the Dordogne?

33rd Day

I needed to talk to someone, so I turned to Bogie. Despite finding it difficult to put up with his farting, I shared a cell with him and there was no one else I could turn to.

He'd been banged up for something much worse than me, which made me feel much better.

In three words.

Simply killing someone.

When he told me this I was incredibly shocked and said that I was not sure I wanted to sleep with him anymore.

I called for a prison officer who told me to shut up, stop complaining, and go to sleep.

34th Day

I received a joint letter from my son and daughter today – James, 26 and Fiona 24 – in which they said they thought I was a disgusting person and that they never wanted to see me again.

I've loved them since they were born, spent a bloody fortune on their education and now I get this. I suppose they're bloody perfect, of course.

I suppose it's true to say that my whole world was crumbling around me.

35th Day

I awoke early, feeling very nervous. I could hear Bogie snoring in the bunk below and the guards' feet echoing about the prison as they patrolled our cells.

I crept out of my bunk as quietly as I could and climbed down the creaking framework, doing my best not to disturb him.

I went to the loo in the corner as quietly as I could and did not flush it in case I should wake him.

When I crept back to our bunks I knelt beside him and looked into his snoring face.

Since living with him for only a few days he had never struck me as a violent person, let alone a murderer, and to be honest he didn't look like one curled up like a baby and sleeping so cosily.

But impressions, let alone first impressions, can be misleading, and when I looked at his hands lying on the pillow beside his cheeks I could see on the knuckles of one the word LOVE and on the other HATE.

36th Day

The days go by slowly here. There's the wake-up call, which is a very loud bell, then showers, and once we have dressed into our prison clothes there is breakfast, which is always absolutely fantastic: eggs, bacon, sausage, fried bread and tomatoes. Also brilliant coffee and beautifully cooled orange juice.

To be honest, I wouldn't have minded if I had to stay here forever. I had no one to go home to and probably no home.

But I could tell Bogie was itching to get out as soon as he could, and because of our newly formed friendship I felt, in a strange way, a premonition, that our chance meeting in one of Her Majesty's best hotels might lead in the most unlikely scenario to something more permanent and mutually beneficial.

37th Day

When the right opportunity arrived I asked Bogie if I could have a word and we sat down on his bunk side by side.

He knew a little of what I'd been going through recently and to be honest he couldn't have cared less. But when I expressed my concern over how I was going to make an income when I left this place he did have a few ideas.

We came from very different backgrounds and his priorities were the total opposite of mine and he was going to be in this place for a lot longer than me, lucky chap.

He did give me some good advice though.

38th Day

I didn't sleep very well last night. Bogie's words were going round and round, echoing in my head, a murderer yes, but such wisdom.

I thought I knew what I had to do when I got out of this place. Yes, I'd thought I would learn plastering however long it took me, but after Bogie's pep talk I had second thoughts. I, with my qualifications and talent, he said, could do better than that.

Now let me tell you the truth of our conversation last night.

Quite simply he told me to start stealing things. Start off small, he said, and then when you get your confidence go for something bigger.

Bogie suggested supermarkets first because, he told me, they were easy. Then try something more daring. With all my connections he said the world was my oyster.

We had some exciting plans for the afternoon.

While a diversion, which consisted of a mass brawl, took place on one side of the prison yard and involved the duties of the prison staff to break it up, tobacco, spirits and drugs were being thrown to the rest of us over the fence on the other side of the prison by prisoners' families and friends into well-practised hands.

My prison colleagues could well have played cricket at Lord's.

39th Day

As I said, if you are well behaved in here you get to join the local community, to start with accompanied by a prison warden, and once you have proved yourself responsible, you are on your own, and if this all goes well an early release is on the cards.

This was my day and I had to sweep the streets of Goudhurst with my warden looking on.

I did not look like I was going to run away so he left me to my sweeping and took his opportunity and walked into the Star and Eagle for a pint.

I knew this was my chance to carry out the advice Bogie had given me.

While sweeping outside the chemist I decided to walk in.

I leant my broom on the window beside the front door and then wandered around the shop a bit and when I thought no one was watching I stole some vitamin C tablets.

I took them off the shelf and put them into my pocket.

I left the chemist hurriedly and nervously and anxiously waited for someone to tap me on the shoulder, but after a few minutes and retrieving my broom I realised I'd got away with it.

The entire episode sent a pleasurable tingle up my spine and left me feeling on a high and wanting more. I had conquered my fear and my adrenaline rush was amazing.

But I also wondered what I was really doing and what was happening to me. This was crazy behaviour. I used to be a judge but now it seemed I had decided my place in the community was on the wrong side of the law.

40th Day

I was still determined to learn this plastering lark so I diligently attended the prison course but laughed smugly to myself about easy money.

Plastering is very difficult and really if you don't have to do it I suggest you don't.

But it was a good way of relaxing in prison while thinking about what I could steal when I got out of here.

Something – I hoped – a little more valuable than a packet of vitamin C tablets.

Having said that, I lay in my bunk bed now, with Bogie sleeping and farting above me, enjoying a lovely mug of fizzing orange goodness. We'd swapped beds because Bogie had told me to. I had kept waking him during the night when going to the loo.

First challenge, first hurdle put to bed.
Oh my goodness!

41st Day

I think this whole process has done me quite a lot of good actually.

I have admitted before that I think I am a bit smug and important and I feel that finally I have been dragged down to Earth, not only by my conscience, my time in prison, but also by the bloody press who have not left me alone, even when behind bars.

Thank goodness Bogie had now nudged me, perhaps in the wrong direction, but onto the first step of the ladder.

I could now boast that I had successfully stolen something.

42nd Day

Like I had predicted, and because of my good behaviour and not having been caught stealing vitamin C tablets from the local chemist, the prison governor called me into his office, escorted by two guards, to inform me I was to be released.

Even I was surprised by this early gift of freedom. I'd hardly been banged up for more than two weeks.

I promised Bogie that I would keep in touch and let him know how my stealing was going, but I probably wouldn't and I doubted whether I would ever see him again.

I hugged him at the gates affectionately and we both looked at each other with mischief in our eyes.

"Goodbye Bogie," I said.

43rd Day

I arrived back at the manor, driven by two jolly nice police officers called Pete and Geoff.

They dropped me off and told me in no uncertain terms to behave myself in the future. A prisoner does not usually be driven by police officers but I assumed it was because I was a very important person.

When I walked through the front door I passed Mrs Jury who was already leaving the hall in a rush with her suitcase.

She was wearing a tee shirt, which on the front said, "Handle with Care – Highly Excitable."

I said, "Hello darling, where are you going?"

And she said, "Why don't you just fuck off and leave me alone, you pervert."

Her eyes were full of hate.

"Is it the French chappy?" I asked, to which she put two fingers up my nose.

A taxi then arrived and she was gone and I could swear, as the taxi disappeared up the drive, I saw her hand showing me two fingers from the back window.

Even so, it felt good to be home.

Despair is not a place I wish to return to. I observe all that I see now and all that happens about me as the next adventure.

For me, the glass is always half full. Fuck the old bat.

I reached for the whiskey bottle.

44th Day

I'm rattling around my huge house now all by myself, apart from the welcome company of my cat.

I've put the manor on the market as nobody wants to live here with me and because I am being sued for a huge amount of money for my groping, or rather what I had been convicted for, yes, assault.

"Absolutely bloody ridiculous," I said to myself while pouring a large glass of claret and lighting a huge Cuban cigar.

I felt I'd earned it.

There are always issues and I now seem to have plenty of them. Deal with them, or simply run away?

Or perhaps because my family have made up their minds about me, it is much easier for me now, because I'm alone.

45th Day

Bogie's suggestion of stealing things kept going round and round in my mind. Even without my judge's income I was a wealthy man and could retire comfortably but this stealing business had fired my imagination and ignited my zest for life. I felt my blood rushing to my head.

So far I had only stolen some vitamin C tablets but he assured me my confidence would grow. And for some reason, it had. I was now racking my brains, trying to think of something bigger and better, something spectacular I could steal.

I'd asked the estate agent to call in the afternoon and when he arrived I spent a whole hour showing him around my estate, explaining in great detail the history of the place and the improvements I had made over the last twenty-five years I'd lived here.

He only valued my impressive stack at five million, so I told him to fuck off. It's worth at least seven.

And that's on a bad day.

46th Day

I got what's-his-name to wash the Bentley this morning, then watched the Six Nations, England v France at Stade de France in Paris in the afternoon.

It was a great result and we thrashed the frogs.

47th Day

I had cabin fever and had to get out of the house, so I decided to go to church, picking up the papers on the way from the post office-cum-village shop.

Apart from myself, who sang my heart out, the rest of the depleted congregation mouthed the words to the hymns and then we were all treated to another boring sermon.

But I must say the vicar had welcomed me with open arms, despite the entire parish knowing of my misdemeanour and my short spell in prison.

So all credit to him, and I tried to concentrate on what he had to say but to be honest I kept drifting off.

During the service, the lady church warden whom I had sat next to at our parish lunch in January kept looking in my direction. I had dismissed her advances then but a lot of things had changed since that day so I gave her a smile, at which she blushed and turned her head away.

I looked at her in a different light now and realised she wasn't that bad looking. I knew she was not married so after the service I invited her back to the manor for lunch.

At lunch, I did most of the talking and she listened intently. Her name is Sally and I made her laugh, at which her face lit up and her eyes went smoky. I was beginning to find her quite sexy and as I was pretty desperate by this time, we ended up in bed for the afternoon.

She said she was impressed with my love-making and I had not heard that compliment for some time.

She was good in bed too and I felt she must have been as desperate as me.

Afterwards we had a glass of champagne and then I drove her home. Before she got out of the car I kissed her goodbye and watched her stride, shaking her arse, towards her cottage.

She gave me a naughty smile as she shut her front door and then I drove home with a contented smile on my face. I didn't feel guilty at all; to be honest I felt chuffed.

48th Day

Having myself contacted an estate agent I regarded with more repute, my house is now on the market for seven and a half million and when I sell it I will be much more comfortable. That fucking woman telephoned me today saying she wants some of my money and I told her to fuck off and live in the bed she had made for herself.

When I sell my house, I will then consider how to invest this money, while continuing to work on my plan to make a lot more.

I gave Sally a call to see how she was, and after a very flirty chat suggested we meet up again soon, in fact, why not come over now.

Our love-making was even better the second time, if that was possible, and when she'd gone home I retired to bed early, thoroughly exhausted.

This was a good way of getting fit; perhaps I might even lose a little weight.

49th Day

I obviously had connections and – apart from my groping issue – people respected me and would confide in me. I was sure given a little time people would forgive my uncharacteristic behaviour and memories would fade.

I was sure.

I had a well-respected career and, although I had now been struck off, my powers of persuasion, influence and intellect would continue to flow amongst the elite of the community.

This, I hoped, would give me the opportunity I was looking for. A chance to mastermind a crime the public would only wonder at. My imagination was running wild and I found it difficult to sleep.

But I did in the end find it and my dreams were of the adrenalin rush I had felt stealing the vitamin C tablets from the chemist and the exciting anticipation surrounding my new but as-yet-undiscovered and mischievous plan.

50th Day

Out of the blue, I had a call from Lord Stinger's secretary asking if I would like to shoot on Friday and, if I wished, join the shooting party tomorrow night for dinner.

The shooting season finishes at the end of January but Lord Stinger, CEO of one of the largest banks in Europe, was a rule unto himself.

Lord Stinger has a huge estate in Lincolnshire, where I had been invited to shoot for many years.

His house is a gigantic pile; the grounds are perfectly beautiful and the surrounding shoot always provides some beautiful birds.

I shoot incredibly well and last year we managed to bag a thousand birds that day and, much to the annoyance of the other guns, I shot most of them. My Purdey had become so hot I could hardly hold it in my hands and my loader admitted to being exhausted from all his stuffing.

I looked forward with relish to dinner the following night and the day's shooting on Friday.

51st Day

My journey up the A1 was effortless. I left the Bentley in the garage and took the Range Rover. It behaved impeccably and I arrived at Lord Stinger's Estate, East Lake Hall, at six-thirty pm.

I left my guns in the boot, locked the car, and with my suitcase in hand walked towards the porch stairs, at which point the front door was opened by his butler.

Stinger, with his faithful springer spaniel called Herbert, greeted me warmly in the hallway and told me dinner would be at eight.

He said he was looking forward to hearing all about my recent adventures, admitting that he had been following my exploits closely in the press but more than anything else he wanted to hear all about it first-hand.

I was then shown to my room for the night by his butler, who took my suitcase from me. But before I mounted the stairs my eyes were drawn to Lord Stinger's dog, and specifically to his collar, which must have been new because I did not remember it from last year.

It looked to me to be studded with shiny stones, possibly even diamonds, and at very regular intervals.

Stinger's butler opened the door to my room and put my case on the bed.

He then asked if there was anything else I required, to which I replied a scotch and water with ice would be nice. He said he would bring it directly, which he did, appearing only a few minutes later with a large tumbler, the ice tinkling against the glass, and presented on a silver tray.

I showered and dressed for dinner, downed my scotch in one and then made my way down the stairs to the drawing room, where the shooting party were drinking champagne.

The men stood in a circle talking loudly, and from what I could gather, about how much money each of them had made recently, each trying to upstage the other with their – I'm sure exaggerated – financial dealings.

Their wives sat on chairs and sofas talking quietly, with the exception of the occasional comment of "Do shut up darling and stop showing off!"

Once they caught sight of me entering the room the loud banter turned to silence.

And then Stinger stepped forward shook my hand and gathered me into the throng, at the same time putting a glass of champagne in my hand.

The banter and laughter began once more while everyone shook my hand and clapped me on the back, demanding to know more about my well-published and despicable antics.

Stinger told them all they would have to wait until dinner. I felt at home and relieved to be made so welcome in such company.

I turned to look at the ladies, each of them bowing their heads, giving me a warm and slightly embarrassed smile.

I then found myself engrossed in conversation with one of the guns who had made his fortune out of recycling old bicycles. He seemed obsessed with me, and with all the guests eager to take their turn in talking to me I felt rather like a celebrity, which I suppose I was.

After a while we made our way through to the dining room, where the table was covered in a damask cloth covered with silver cutlery, china and two candles with golden flames, and upon the walls hung pictures by Andy Warhol and Picasso and I eyed them all enviously as the lightning thought shot through my head. How could I steal them?

We were all shown to our places and sat down. To my left the chair was empty and I wondered why until the door to the kitchen opened and a woman entered gracefully, perching herself beside me.

The room fell silent.

It was the woman I had groped in the Guildhall. She turned to look at me and smiled, her cheeks a deep crimson. And then Stinger stood at the head of the table and raised his glass saying, "To outrageous behaviour!"

Stinger had set me up but it did not seem to matter; everyone was smiling at me and the laughing did not stop.

Despite this woman suing me for a fortune she still had beautifully large breasts and was entirely vulnerable. I could see now why after too much claret I could have done what I did.

I kissed her on the cheek, much to the astonishment of the gathering, and we had a marvellous evening together, talking about my indiscretion, and I said I was very sorry.

Once more I held court, telling my adventures to the guests around the table, who hung on my every word.

Being in the dock and being in prison was something these successful people had never experienced and they were fascinated by my stories, even though much of what I recounted had been covered extensively in the press. But I did not reveal my newfound obsession with stealing things, as this might involve several of the people who sat around the table that evening listening to me.

52nd Day

I awoke this morning to the sound of birds twittering, and the sun's rays arched through the bedroom window between the colourfully embroidered curtains onto what had been a very comfortable bed. I had a sip of whiskey from my flask and jumped out of bed, ready for a new day.

I had slept well, and after a quick shower I put on my tweeds and went down to join the rest of the guns for breakfast. Unlike last night there was not the banter of last night's dinner, and I put this down to everyone having a hangover.

After breakfast I retrieved my Purdey and cartridge bag from the boot of my Range Rover and put them over my shoulders.

We all gathered in front of Stinger's pile, the dogs excitedly rushing about us, their tails wagging furiously.

Stinger then approached each gun with a leather pouch from which nine ivory pegs stood proud and I drew stand number seven.

We were told to move up two after each drive and not to shoot any white pheasants. A whistle would be blown at the end of each drive.

All the guns looked splendid in their checked shirts, ties, caps and tweeds but I had intended to look the most flamboyant in my regalia, which I think I achieved.

Some of the guns were already taking swigs of their fancy from their hip flasks, which I guessed must have been a hair-of-the-dog remedy.

And talking of dogs, I noticed Herbert was not the only dog to have a sparkly studded collar; they were obviously all the rage.

There was also Sir Alfred MacLostit, who was in property and his dog, a brown and white Jack Russell called Rusty, and a black Labrador with a beautiful shiny coat that belonged to Sir Gerald Watson, a stockbroker, and both sported sparkling studded collars.

Perhaps, should the stones be real diamonds, this was not such a bad idea.

After all, securing the safe keeping of these precious stones, should they be precious stones, what stranger, what diamond thief even, would risk being bitten while trying to remove a collar from a dog?

Lord Stinger owed me the odd favour due to important legal things I had done for him in the past and I supposed that is why I had been invited.

Herbert, his faithful Springer Spaniel, chose, much to Stinger's displeasure, to rush to my side and sit at my feet. This gave me a chance to look more closely at his diamond-studded collar. I was no expert, but to me, they looked like the real deal.

And then I glanced across at the beaters and there in their midst of them stood Bogie looking just the part in country tweeds.

He had been released for good behaviour, despite having murdered someone, and had tracked me down by means of Facebook and quizzing the woodcutter in my garden.

Flabbergasted, I called him over and asked him to carry my gun and cartridges. He would be my loader for the day and I told him I had a plan.

Now, Herbert would be an easy dog to kidnap because he was a springer spaniel and very gentle and friendly, and to Lord Stinger's annoyance seemed to totally adore me.

As usual, I shot brilliantly, although I could not, to my neighbouring guns' disgust, stop myself taking the occasional bird which was not mine, and the woman who I had groped and had sat next to during the dinner the night before, could not stop herself giving me admiring glances.

Bogie loaded brilliantly and I guessed this was not the first time he had been so close to a gun.

We stopped for silver tumblers of sloe gin mid-morning and the lunch was grand, during which the loud banter of the evening before once more returned.

We had two drives in the afternoon, at which Herbert was itching to run to my side but was restrained by Stinger who was becoming intensely annoyed by his dog's affection for me.

We had six drives and the bag for the day was 649.

After tea, during which the dogs all begged for a piece of cake – including Herbert, who rested his head upon my foot – I thanked my host for a wonderful day, bade farewell to the other guests and made my way from the drawing room, into the hall, down the marble steps and across the gravel to join Bogie who was waiting for me beside the Range Rover.

But it was not until I was halfway towards my car that I realised Herbert was at my heels.

I glanced over my shoulder to check no one was watching while Bogie opened the Range Rover's tailgate.

Then together we just lifted Herbert into the boot of the Range Rover and shut the tailgate.

Bogie and I then threw the doors of the Range Rover open, got in, slammed them shut in unison and drove off, disappearing down the gravel drive in a cloud of dust, heading hurriedly towards the A1.

Bogie drove smoothly and I slept all the way home. This stealing lark was sweet.

53rd Day

I awoke, having enjoyed a good night's sleep, exhausted from the previous day's shooting, with Herbert lying at the foot of my bed.

I ached a little after all the walking and my right shoulder was bruised as a result of the continuous backlash from the stock of my gun as, greedy as I am, I shot every bird that came anywhere near me.

Bogie had slept the night in one of the manor guest rooms, which, after returning home from prison, I had decorated rather badly in lots of plaster and green paint. I had still not got this plastering technique off to a tee. The room is far away from mine so I couldn't smell or hear him farting.

My mobile began ringing. I picked it up from my bedside table, unplugged the charging cable and put it to my ear.

It was Lord Stinger, who asked me if I had stolen his dog.

I said no, of course not, why should I have done?

When I hung up I gave Herbert a big hug, rolled over to the other side of my bed with him in my arms, staring at what I was sure was a diamond-studded collar, and went back to sleep.

Herbert did not seem to be bothered in the least about being kidnapped, in fact, for some reason I did not understand, he seemed to love me. We had an affinity; perhaps it was my smell? I did not know, but I was sure that if Herbert was a cat he would be purring.

Let Lord Stinger sweat, I thought. I was on a roll.

54th Day

We all went to church today: Bogie, Herbert and me. On the way I suggested to Bogie that he should take this opportunity to say a little prayer and ask forgiveness for his simply horrific sins. I said this with a tiny pinch of salt but it gave him something to think about.

I glanced at him from the driver's seat and told him he looked absolutely splendid in one of my old suits, which fitted him rather well. It showed that I really had put a lot of weight on over the years, because Bogie was as lean and fit as a butcher's dog.

Sally was in church as I expected, so I asked her to join us for lunch at our local, The Bull and Gate, where they serve an excellent Sunday roast.

The pub was packed but I was able to secure my favourite table in the corner, where we enjoyed each other's amusing stories as well as delicious roast beef and Yorkshire pudding while Herbert lay, incredibly well behaved, at our feet. Bogie must have been hungry; I've never seen someone eat so fast.

55th Day

I awoke late; it was becoming a bit of a habit, but after all I had nothing else to do, no train to catch, no Old Bailey and no dishing out life sentences to look forward to. I had to admit I was enjoying my new lifestyle. It was completely different in every way and I felt refreshed.

And then my mobile rang.

It was my estate agent telling me that they had received an offer on the manor.

He mentioned a figure of six and a half million and I told him to fuck off and then shut my phone off for the rest of the day.

In the afternoon I approached Bogie who was digging the beds and pruning roses in the garden. He had not been his usual self at lunchtime and I wondered what was wrong. I put my hand on his shoulder and asked him if he needed to talk. He immediately went down to his knees and began to sob uncontrollably. What is it, I asked anxiously, and in between deep sobs, he muttered the words, "I didn't mean to kill him, I just had to shut him up and then he was dead, dead in my arms…"

56th Day

Herbert, Bogie and I were getting on famously: long walks together, throwing sticks and tennis balls, which Herbert loved chasing and we spoiled him rotten with the most expensive dog meals we could find in Waitrose.

Bogie was back to his usual self today. All I could think of saying to him yesterday was that it must be a hard thing to live with. He explained that it had happened while trying to rob a drug dealer in Ealing and that he punched the guy too hard.

Lord Stinger had put an advert in the Times offering a reward of £10,000 to anyone who could shed light on where Herbert was.

He would have to do better than that.

57th Day

Today I took Herbert's collar off and asked Bogie to make a visit to Garrard in Albemarle Street to have the stones valued. A little risky I know. He could scarper with the proceeds, but this was not only a valuation but also a test of his loyalty.

When removing the collar I discovered a silver locket attached, which I found hidden beneath his fur.

When Bogie had left for London with the collar I undid the clasp of the locket and pulled out a tiny curled piece of parchment.

On this, written in elegant scrawl, was a six-digit sort code, followed by a sixteen-digit account number to a Swiss bank account and, miraculously, a user name and password and most notably the all-important pass code, which replaced the account holder's name and gave the account holder the desired anonymity and of course, access to the money. The bank's name was Geneva Central AG.

The rest was easy, I simply logged in on my laptop and within a couple of minutes I was looking at Lord Stinger's account details and a balance of 565,000,000 Swiss Francs, which in our money amounted to some 400,000,000 pounds Sterling.

I had opened a Swiss bank account many years ago so I knew the login process well. The next thing I did was to transfer 95,000,000 Swiss Francs – I didn't want to be greedy – into my Swiss account and hope no one, particularly Lord Stinger would notice.

Bogie phoned me from the train back from London telling me he'd got £26,450 for Herbert's collar and would be back about six. I said that was great and I would treat him for dinner at The Bull and Gate to celebrate. I added that I thought we better find ourselves another dog.

58th Day

I haven't got to sell the manor anymore and I have changed all the locks so that cow Mrs Jury and my despicable children cannot get in.

I knew that Sir Alfred MacLostit had another huge pile with lots of land around it and, of course, he had a dog with a diamond collar. And he had no respect for the shooting calendar either.

Despite my humiliation over my well-publicised groping episode and my time in prison I put on a brave face and rang him up to arrange a day's shooting.

Surprisingly, he was almost ecstatic to hear from me; told me to come tomorrow, that one of the guns had cancelled because his wife was having an emergency hysterectomy, and so it was booked.

I was on a roll and I felt good fortune was at my heels.

59th Day

Seven am and we were off, Bogie driving very smoothly in the Range Rover.

We both sipped coffee from a flask, mine topped up with Scotch, and Herbert, whom I'd had re-sprayed so no one – and particularly Lord Stinger – would recognise him, sat in the back.

He used to be a black and white springer; he was now, thanks to Bogie's handiwork, brown and white.

It was a great day and I think we shot another thousand birds. I shot most of them and Herbert was brilliant, picking up wonderfully and no one recognised him, not even Lord Stinger who shot dreadfully as usual, which was a pleasure for me to see. It is also worth mentioning Herbert showed no interest at all in his previous owner.

We stayed the night at Sir Alfred MacLostit's estate and the evening and dinner were fantastic.

Bogie had supper in the kitchen with the cooks and slept in the servants' quarters.

As soon as we arrived this dog came bounding towards me and jumped into my arms. It was Rusty, the Jack Russell who belonged to Sir Alfred MacLostit, and I loved him immediately. More importantly he still sported a magnificent collar, studded with what I assumed would be, once more, diamonds. I was sure they were; after all, I was becoming a bit of an expert at recognising them.

60th Day

I don't think Herbert was too bothered when Bogie lifted Rusty into the boot of the Range Rover to join him in the morning because they had both got on famously together; Herbert trying to do a good job picking up pheasants while Rusty, his teeth snarling, trying to pinch them from him. Typical Jack Russell.

We were then off at speed before Sir Alfred could wonder where Rusty had gone.

The A1 beckoned and Bogie floored it while Herbert and Rusty, who had both jumped onto the back seat, leant expertly left and then right into the sways of the gentle country bends.

When we got home Rusty jumped onto my lap as Bogie lit the fire in the drawing room. The arrival of a second dog was too much for my beloved cat who, despite that it was pouring with rain, scarpered the minute we walked through the door.

We'd picked up a takeaway curry, which we devoured while nibbling on poppadoms and enjoyed a documentary on the Spitfire.

Our new dog also had a clasp beneath his diamond collar, which I carefully unscrewed to reveal another piece of parchment upon which were Sir Alfred MacLostit's Swiss bank account details.

Only this time I would not be able to access the account unless I flew to Switzerland with Rusty and used his paw on a pad.

These pads were used for fingerprint identification and Sir Alfred had decided that Rusty's paw was the key.

61st Day

When we got to the airport, I put Rusty in a bag, zipped it up, said goodbye to Bogie who was going to use his time to cash in Rusty's collar at Garrard's, checked in, and I didn't seem to have any problem walking through customs, passport control and into the aircraft.

I took my usual seat at the back of the plane, and even though Rusty was struggling slightly I just gave him a rub and then he was OK and no one seemed to notice, even though he made the occasional whine.

Once we got to 35,000 feet I asked for my usual gin and tonic and also a biscuit I would give to Rusty when none of the cabin crew were looking.

We dropped into Geneva with a bump and then later on I found myself sitting opposite this stunningly attractive Swiss banker who looked slightly curious as to why I was clutching a Jack Russell. She sat behind this enormous desk and looked quite pleased to see me.

I handed my bank details to her and explained that Rusty needed to put his paw on the pad to identify him and as a result allow the money to be transferred to my bank account. These dogs are quite useful aren't they?

I walked from the bank absolutely ecstatic, with the transfer complete and the Alps all around us. The sun was shining and I felt happy. Rusty had made me another £45 million.

I thought I'd go and have a wonderful lunch at Bistro de la Tour, one of my favourite restaurants in Geneva, and the staff were quite happy for Rusty to sit at my feet.

Rusty and I ate well and then laughed and barked all the way back to our hotel.

62nd Day

Today Bogie re-sprayed Rusty, who now became not a brown and white Jack Russell but a black and white Jack Russell, using some hair dye he'd picked up from Boots.

I don't think I can be bothered to kidnap another dog; after all I don't really need to.

All I had to do was find myself a new wife. I had over £100 million in the bank and after all my hard work I thought I deserved a holiday.

I knew exactly where I was going to go: my favourite place, Saint Tropez in the South of France.

I'd been on holiday there since I was a boy and absolutely loved the place.

I would fly out tomorrow and Bogie could look after the dogs.

63rd Day

I love Nice Airport.

When the plane lands here and I smell France I am in heaven. I have a window seat and during the plane's approach it always looks like we are going to land in the sea.

I wanted to spend a lot of money because I had a lot of money.

I had arranged the hire of a Ferrari California, which was there waiting for me in front of the airport terminal. It had only cost me 8000 euros for seven days, which I considered a bargain.

A very pleasant monsieur handed me the keys and I was off at great speed, deciding to take the twisting coast road and take in the scenery and scent of the Cote d'Azur and to enjoy of course this fantastic car.

I'd booked the Byblos and when I got to my bedroom I ordered the largest Sunseeker they could deliver straight away and then sent out an invite to all my friends on Facebook to come on board. It would be great to meet them and find out, finally, who they all were.

After I had done this, I wished I hadn't. Claret not to blame this time but an extremely good burgundy.

64th Day

Jolly hot down here for this time of year and only 45 of my Facebook friends have taken up my invitation, thank goodness, so I have a fleet of taxis bringing them all from the airport to the hotel.

I've reserved all their rooms but I'm not sure whether we will all be able to get onto my boat, even though it's 75 feet long and cost me a fucking fortune.

65th Day

I was not completely confident in how to drive this bloody thing and my guests, or should I call them my passengers, looked very worried.

I managed to steer the beautiful but fucking enormous boat out of Saint Tropez harbour and headed for Pampelonne beach and Le Club 55 where I had booked a table for 46.

Lunch was as always truly fantastic.

I just loved sitting there wiggling the sand between my toes and looking at all the successful people, like me, on the tables around me.

I knew some of my guests, but some – who were jolly nice people – I had no idea who they were but they insisted they were my friends so I went along with it.

Afterwards we all went swimming and then had showers under the wicker compartments.

I then decided I would take them back to Saint Tropez and tell them all to fuck off.

66th Day

They have now all gone, thank goodness, and I'm now reclining by the pool thinking about how rich I am.

I've had my eye out for a new woman and I think I might have just spotted her.

I'm a bit tubby so when it comes to women I'm not as confident as when I'm in court or kidnapping dogs.

Anyway I was going to have a go, after all she looked gorgeous.

I walked towards her to introduce myself, tripped, and luckily fell into the pool, in so doing I miraculously did the most magnificent dive. When I surfaced she was looking at me with complete amazement and admiration.

I struggled out of the pool and asked her to have a drink with me at the bar. I was very pleased when she smiled and said yes.

We sat at the bar watching everyone swimming, sunbathing and talking and it just seemed to me that we were meant for each other.

We hit it off immediately. Her husband had just died, thank goodness, and she was also very pretty and I could picture her in my manor cooking me bangers and mash in the kitchen wearing high heels and not much else except for an apron.

I knew what I liked and how to go about getting it.

When I got back to my room I gave Bogie a ring to see how things were going and he was in Waitrose buying more dog food.

I'd arranged to have lunch with this delicious woman at Le Club 55.

We would go in my new Ferrari, which was parked in the underground car park. I'd booked the table for one o'clock.

When we got there the place was buzzing and totally packed.

I parked the Ferrari under the large canopy and I held her hand and walked in past the kitchen and the beautiful aromas.

We were shown by Patrice to our table after our host had given us both too many kisses.

What's the matter with these French people?

67th Day

Lying by the pool at the Byblos now with my new lady, whose name is Louise, pretending to read a book but at every opportunity glancing at her in her bikini; she is gorgeous. I haven't got into her knickers yet but I am looking forward to it.

I've got rid of that bloody boat; I do not have the courage to drive the fucking thing anymore and I am beginning to scare people, plus the cost of mooring it in the harbour is horrific.

68th Day

Still lying by the pool and despite my efforts have still not got into Louise's knickers.

I'm not very good at this type of thing but trust me I will get there, even if I have to pay her.

69th Day

She was French and sometimes I found it difficult to understand what she was talking about but that didn't matter because she had the most fantastic arse.

She also, during a conversation at dinner, told me that her dead husband used to be in oil; in fact he had owned an oil company, which was now hers.

I must admit my desire to make this woman my next wife had gone through the roof.

70th Day

Hotel Byblos, situated at the centre of Saint Tropez, is a beacon for the international jet set. Just minutes away from the port with its fishing boats and pleasure craft and the world-famous beaches, the hotel offers all the charm of a real village, designed in 1967 in pure Mediterranean style. The most recent room (built in 2003) is a suite of 180 m² overlooking the pool, available as separate modules or as a whole. This sunny suite comprises a large living room and two bedrooms, one with a private terrace.

That's what it said in the brochure anyway which I close and toss to the end of my bed as my new girlfriend sleeps peacefully beside me.

I am staying in this room which, I must admit, is pure luxury.

I still find my new girlfriend difficult to understand. I can speak a little French but she talks too quickly and I think she probably does it on purpose. When I get my way, I'll teach her.

71st Day

I got into her knickers this morning and I would like to tell you it was absolutely fantastic. She whispered lovely naughty French things to me as well, which added to my pleasure. Afterwards I had a wonderful hot shower and used lots of shampoo.

72nd Day

I lay by the pool once more feeling completely satisfied. Louise lay next to me and I kept looking at her. It's a shame I'm so tubby and I will have to start running more. Anyway, for the time being, I thought I would order another bottle of champagne.

73ʳᵈ **Day**

I spoke to Bogie this morning; he was walking the dogs and he told me just to continue to enjoy myself and all was fine back at the manor. I went along with his advice and booked a table at Le Club 55. Louise gave me a naughty smile and we fell into bed.

Le Club 55 was packed again and Louise and I sat at my favourite table in the corner watching successful people enjoying themselves while we both sipped a beautifully chilled burgundy. We nibbled at their famous burnt bread, which I think is vastly overrated and with the aromas of the kitchen drifting towards us we were looking forward to our monkfish, which was delicious.

After lunch we made our way to the beach where I asked this young muscled French chappy for two mattresses and a sun shade. We had a lovely lazy afternoon, sunbathing, swimming and reading our books.

74ᵗʰ **Day**

I worry about death but there is no point. There is nothing before you are born and nothing after you die. It's like going to sleep. All you can do is make the most of your time and enjoy it while you can; it's the same for all of us. I go to church on Sundays because I always have. Since a boy at school I have made this weekly ritual seeking inspiration but never finding it.

I showered and dressed and then rushed down for breakfast. We'd had quite an active night.

I was hungry, yes, but not for Louise's fortune, she was too good for that. I was looking, despite the holiday atmosphere, for someone else and something much bigger.

After breakfast, I persuaded Louise to come with me and we headed for the Eglise Paroissiale Notre Dame de l'Assomption on the Rue Commandant Guichard. The

Baroque architecture is breathtaking and the organ painted in green is beautiful.

After the service, I left this place feeling inspired. At home Christians are meant to forgive. But here, in the land of Catholicism, there is nothing like hell and high water to get you looking over your shoulder.

Louise then pulled me by the hand and guided us towards Le Girelier to have lunch and enjoy the view of the harbour and the super yachts, the Harley Davidsons growling by, and all the beautiful people dressed in cotton with an outline of an alligator tattooed on their ankle wandering the promenade.

75th Day

This holidaying stuff was all very well but I was getting a bit itchy to make some more money.

Funnily enough I think I might have something on the go. There's this chap from England staying in the hotel, and no he has not got a dog but he does fancy my new girlfriend, bastard. I have just thought to myself, I will put this to my advantage. I am not sure how yet but I am working on it. His name is Christopher Nelson.

76th Day

I awoke with a start early and left Louise sleeping and wandered down to the harbour to have a coffee at the Senequier. The day was still quiet and peaceful and not yet disturbed by beautiful people, motorbikes, expensive cars and mega rich egos on their gin palaces who were still sleeping.

After my coffee, I walked through the damp fish market hidden behind the Senequier under an archway and bought some fish.

I was excited because I had another plan and it involved this chap, Christopher Nelson, who fancied my new girlfriend.

77th Day

This chap, Christopher Nelson, really annoyed me.

Admittedly I had not known Louise that long but I considered her mine and what right did he have to think he could take her behind my back?

None.

I suppose I'm a jealous sort of chap but I can't stand these bastards who think they can just take your woman because they think they are so fucking charismatic and can charm and win whichever woman they want.

This guy can just simply fuck off or I am going to arrange a nasty surprise for him. I am good at that.

78th Day

Yes, there he was again, sniffing around my new girlfriend as we lay by the pool.

He had some very tight blue swimming trunks on and to be honest his figure was much better than mine and I hated him for it.

I got up from my sunbed and walked towards the hotel and accidently knocked him into the pool, at least that's what I wanted everyone to think.

When he came to the surface he screamed some expletives at me, most referring to me being a very fat person.

79th Day

I went onto Facebook this morning and found this very infuriating chap looking very smug, with a profile picture of him in his blue swimming trunks.

By looking at his timeline I was able to discover lots about him, and knowledge is king.

He was quite rich, worth about 200 million pounds. I got this information from doing a Google on him.

From the pictures on Facebook it was obvious he liked women and was an extraordinary flirt. Divorced for the third time, he was now single again, which he put out there onto the social media cloud. He was a commodity broker and he specialised in gold.

80th Day

Now those fish I bought from the market behind the Senequier I gave to the hotel chef and I now told him I would like them cooked for me tonight.

They were deliciously fresh and smelt lovely; these monkfish are gorgeous and although I knew the restaurant could provide their own, I had taken great pleasure in buying them myself from the market and the chef agreed with great enthusiasm to prepare them for me.

I decided to go for a run. Christopher Nelson's outbursts about my shape had hit home and I needed to do something about it so I ran all the way to Pampelonne beach and arrived at Club 55, only to see Christopher Nelson standing at the bar in his tight blue swimming trunks.

During my run an idea had come to me. My plan might have been a bit ambitious but I thought it could work. As I had discovered, Christopher Nelson was a gambler and a very successful commodity broker and he had a love for gold. All I had to do was tempt him.

I asked him if he would like a drink as I sat down beside him, sweating in my Lycras.

He was just finishing the last drop of what looked like a whiskey and soda.

I ordered two glasses of champagne and we clinked them together and started laughing for some reason, I did not know why, other than that, he was laughing at me in my Lycras and I at him, sitting there in his tight blue swimming trunks.

He was lean and fit and his face was unshaven and very bronzed and he had intense blue eyes that looked at me in a way that unnerved me. He was confident, of course, he had to be, and he'd made a fortune in gold and knew how to seduce women. Perhaps he could see how hopeless I was at seducing women and that was why he was laughing at me?

We exchanged numbers.

81st Day

When I got back to the Byblos, I rang Bogie and, after enquiring after the dogs, asked him if he knew someone who could create a website for Golden Mines. I thought the name was quite brilliant, I'd thought of it on my run, a fictional company of course, that had struck gold, and when I say gold I mean a lot of gold.

I told him it had to be very convincing and done very quickly.

This, he told me, would be surprisingly easy and he knew just the man. The wonder of cutting and pasting, he added.

82nd Day

I telephoned Christopher Nelson from my room this morning and asked him if he would like to meet me for lunch. He sounded surprised, and when I mentioned I had an interesting and potentially very lucrative investment opportunity he sounded intrigued. And when I added that it involved gold I heard a sharp intake of breath at the other end of the line.

I told him to meet at Club 55 at one o'clock and not to wear those blue swimming trunks.

He arrived in some bright fluorescent yellow ones instead.

He joined me at my table where I sat looking splendid in a cream cotton suit with a colourful silk handkerchief poking out of my jacket breast pocket and a fluorescent green and white cravat about my neck.

I had told Louise to go and get her hair done and I didn't want him flirting with her anyway. This was business. As he sat down, I said to hot pants, at least put a tee shirt on, which he did, looking slightly embarrassed, retrieving one from his satchel.

We had two glasses of chilled burgundy and sardines accompanied by some awkward moments of silence, followed by a salad Niçoise, and then I got down to the point.

I leant down and removed from my Gucci briefcase at my feet a bar of gold, which I had picked up from Societe Generale on Boulevard Vasserot, and put it on the table in front of him.

I explained that I had invested in a gold mine in Australia and that we had struck gold big time.

I was banking on him not going to have a look at the mine in person because Australia is such a fucking long way away.

I told him to have a look at the Golden Mines website, which he couldn't do quickly enough, retrieving his mobile from his satchel.

He scrolled up and down, left and right, his eyes eating up the company's information. The history, the accounts, estimated gold reserves, the directors, of which I was of course one, and the images looked very impressive. Bogie had done an excellent job and hot pants looked more than interested.

I told him not to rush into any risky decisions and to sleep on it.

83rd Day

He fell for it.

He called me this morning wanting some of the action. I could not believe how easy it was. It seemed this smart commodity investor had fallen, lock stock and barrel, into my net.

I was lying by the pool with Louise at the Byblos, thinking of my next move and waiting for him to arrive to conclude the deal. I had ordered champagne, three glasses, and a bowl of olives, which the waiter had placed on the table between our sun loungers.

The yarn I had fed him yesterday had got him hooked; I could tell by the look in his eyes.

When he arrived by the pool in his fluorescent blue swimwear I poured him a glass of champagne and explained that if he wished to invest he would have to decide quickly as I had received a call this morning from another potential investor who wanted to take up the balance of the remaining shares in the company. Which I, of course, hadn't, but this really got him going.

He wanted to know immediately how much this other investor was going to put in and when I told him 50 million he started choking on the olive he had just put into his mouth.

I hoped I hadn't pushed my luck too far but he did eventually recover his composure.

I wondered whether his decision to invest might have had something to do with Louise being a distraction, as during our discussions he kept looking at her sunbathing in her bikini beside us.

Bastard.

84th Day

I'm not stupid you know, I used to be a judge after all before I was struck off and I of course knew that if this scam came off, or even if it didn't, I would have to make a run for it, scarper, and pretty quick, because hot pants here would be after me and I could imagine he could call up some pretty nasty henchmen.

I wasn't sure whether I would take Louise with me, I didn't want to put her in danger for one, and secondly she would hold me up. I'm not saying I'm a complete coward but to leave her behind was probably the best idea.

85th Day

I was sitting in La Table du Marche on the Rue des Commerçants waiting for Mr Hot Pants to arrive for lunch.

I was going to order the scrambled eggs with sea urchins and I was going to suggest Christopher Nelson went for the same. I was certainly not going to go for the Moroccan-style lamb. It would bring back rather wrenching memories of Mrs Jury's and my brief excursion to that part of the world.

I'd just ordered a glass of champagne and had my laptop with me and when Christopher Nelson did arrive I pretended to be engrossed in the Golden Mines website.

He looked over my shoulder at my laptop. I asked him to sit down and I ordered him a glass of champagne and recommended the scrambled eggs. "Yes," he said.

I could tell he was eager because he was early, and not only that but he also had his chequebook in hand. But who has a chequebook these days? Only dinosaurs.

I told him in no uncertain terms that I would not accept a cheque from him in 65 million years.

"How do I know I can trust you?" he asked.

"Because I'm a judge," I said, and that seemed to do the trick.

So while we talked about all the money we were going to make he logged into his bank account on his mobile and asked me to witness the transaction.

It was done and it took all my willpower not to let him see me shake when we both tucked into our scrambled eggs.

86th Day

Now, armed with his £50 million I was going to get running.

I checked out of the Byblos, and then, as I'd returned the Ferrari to the hire company, headed for Nice Airport in a taxi, leaving Louise asleep and sunbathing by the pool.

I told the taxi driver to drive as fast as he could.

The EasyJet Boeing 737 took off into the Cote d'Azur sky and as soon as I could, after the plane banked steeply to the right, I ordered a double gin and tonic.

I wondered how much time I had before Christopher Nelson would realise what I had done. Anyway I did not intend to wait around to find out.

I was off.

I was flying into London Gatwick but I had no intention of going home to my manor. As we got to 35 thousand feet and I was tucking into one of their sandwiches I impulsively decided I would take a train to Wales. It was one of the last places anyone would look for me. After all no one goes there unless they have to.

If I was to go home I knew he would find me sooner rather than later with his henchmen.

I would let Bogie know and if they turned up at the manor I wondered whether Bogie might be able to murder them all.

I would ask him.

The good news about all of this though was that I was now worth a staggering amount of money.

When I arrived at Gatwick I ran to show them my passport and then caught the Gatwick Express to London and was soon on a train from Paddington to Swansea. I resisted going to the bar; I needed all my wits about me.

When I got to Swansea Station I hailed a taxi and I did not care how much it would cost.

I was heading for a little village near Aberystwyth called Machynlleth, which lay beside the River Dyfi and it was according to my Google search an incredibly quiet, dreary grey and damp place. Just the place I was looking for.

Just what I needed to steady my nerves and think what I would do next to protect myself. I'm rich and, even I must admit, a bit daring, but – like any other person would be – absolutely terrified.

The taxi cost a bloody fortune but it didn't bother me, I even gave him a tip.

I'm staying at Glandyfi Castle, which is a wonderful place. I'm now relaxing in my room and enjoying the beautiful views of the countryside through the window. I can see the Dyfi estuary from the comfort of my bed and warmed by a little log-burning stove.

The staff gave me a warm welcome and I'm now enjoying delicious Welsh lamb, roast potatoes and spinach with a glass of Australian red wine on a tray and then it will be bed.

Before I slept I phoned Bogie to tell him what I was up to and ask after the dogs. He told me not to worry and said he would put some defence precautions in place around the manor. Nasty stuff, he called it.

I will pull the covers over my head tonight.

87th Day

This morning I had a splendid breakfast.

I opted for boiled eggs and soldiers which I enjoyed in the restaurant with some deliciously strong coffee. It was just what I needed.

The other hotel guests at the tables all around me kept giving me, "don't I know you?" looks, as they sat not knowing what to say to each other.

I know I cannot stay here forever.

Or perhaps I could?

I telephoned Bogie to check that all was well at the manor and that the dogs were fine.

He assured me all was tight and cool and he was about to take them for another walk and then go to Waitrose to get them some more food.

When I returned to my bedroom, I noticed I had received several missed calls from Christopher Nelson.

I did not return them but instead reached for my whiskey bottle.

I telephoned my bank just to make sure Christopher Nelson's transfer was now safely in my account and they assured me it was.

88th Day

Bogie telephoned me early this morning sounding very concerned.

He told me this chap, Christopher Nelson, had called the house phone – I wondered how he had got the number – and wanted to ask me some more questions about Golden Mines and that he was finding it impossible to reach me on my mobile phone.

Bogie told me that he had assured Mr Nelson that at the earliest opportunity he would ask me to return his call.

I was grateful to have Bogie, he was reliable, my friend, knew how to clean my house and walk the dogs, but more importantly he knew how to kill people, which might come in quite useful.

89th Day

I decided that I must call Christopher Nelson and keep him stringing along, otherwise he might become suspicious.

I spoke to him and explained that I had unexpectedly had to return to the UK for very important business reasons and apologised for the delay in returning his calls and after a few more reassurances he sounded satisfied with this explanation.

I was not certain but I thought I could hear Louise's voice whispering French things in the background.

Bastard.

90th Day

This will not surprise you, I went to church today.

St Peter's church in Machynlleth has a spectacular stained glass window but a slightly out-of-tune organ.

Anyway I felt better with myself on leaving and decided to go to the pub and I chose the Red Lion.

Someone at the bar recognised me, probably from my groping incident, which was of course reported widely in the newspapers and asked me did I know what:

LLANFAIRPWLLGWYNGYLLGOGERYCHWYRND ROBWLLLLANTYSYLIOGOGOGOCH

(Something like that) meant and asked me aggressively to repeat it.

I said I did not care what it meant and that I had no intention of repeating it and asked him politely to leave me alone in peace to sup my beer at the bar.

It was not long before I had a large crowd of people around me telling me I was an upper-class English pervert.

I finished my beer and left the pub in a hurry, shutting the pub door with relief and a slam, leaving the abusive language behind me. I had decided that I hated the Welsh more than any other people.

It never stopped raining here and the miserable weather complemented their chip-on-the-shoulder attitudes.

91st Day

I'd been here for six days now and had become bored out of my head.

I'd had enough of the constant rain, the peculiar accents and the fact that there was nothing to do unless you liked climbing mountains.

I felt I must leave and creep back to the manor.

I wasn't looking forward to the journey; it takes forever to get here and even longer to leave.

92nd Day

Bogie picked me up from the station and then it was only a fifteen-minute drive back to the manor.

The dogs were very pleased to see me and the house looked immaculate. It was a relief to be back in civilisation.

Bogie was intrigued to hear all about my exploits and, to be honest, he looked very proud of me.

Both Herbert and Rusty made a complete fuss of me.

It was lovely to be home.

93rd Day

I have got very good security here at the manor: electric reinforced gates, high walls all round, numerous alarms and security lights, a moat, and of course two dogs, as well as the ace in my pack, Bogie.

So I slept well last night.

It was lovely climbing into the clean sheets of my own bed and being home and incredibly rich.

I know I had poked a hornets' nest but I felt if, or rather when, Christopher Nelson came looking for me, this was, after all, the best and safest place to be.

94th Day

Just to be sure though, today I asked a private security company to come round and give me a quote for supplying a number of armed security guards and plenty of land mines as well as electric fencing to be installed all around the manor.

They certainly know how to charge, but I said I wanted it done and they said they would arrive tomorrow with a team of so-called experts to dig in the land mines and install the electric fencing. I would tell them all to report to Bogie.

95th Day

They arrived early in three plain white vans and they all jumped out immediately, opened the rear doors, and set to work.

I told Bogie to go and sort them out and show them where they were staying in the converted stables.

They were all, as I had requested, carrying handguns in their holsters and machine guns hung over their shoulders as well as several hand grenades attached to the belt around their waists.

They worked incessantly from seven o'clock in the morning installing the electric fencing and Bogie instructed the guards where to stand: two at the main entrance and the others positioned strategically around the manor.

Bogie pointed out to me we could be attacked from above by helicopter so I ordered a shoulder-fired rocket launcher, which I was assured would be delivered tomorrow. Thank goodness Amazon don't just sell books anymore!

You could argue I was being a little over-cautious but I thought it better to be safe than sorry.

96ᵗʰ Day

I was very impressed with the rocket launcher, which was delivered this morning.

It was a RPG-7 AT and apparently is the 'default' rocket launcher. I read the brochure thoroughly.

It can lock onto tracer darts and performs well against armour. Its performance is average against infantry and average against buildings but the most important thing is it performs well against helicopters and usually one shot brings them down or knocks them out of control. I placed this killing machine in the hands of Bogie.

97ᵗʰ Day

I got a call this morning from Christopher Nelson and he sounded very angry.

He asked me when the shares in Golden Mines were going to be floated on the market and I said any day now.

I explained we'd had a board meeting yesterday and the date of the company's floatation on the London Stock Exchange would be announced shortly.

He said, "You better not be fucking me around with this fatso because I'll come and get you."

I felt a shiver go down my spine, but still, and perhaps foolishly, before I put the phone down said, "Well you better make sure you're not wearing your tight blue swimming trunks then."

The manor was a fortress; let him come, I thought, as I snuggled up with Herbert in bed. Rusty slept with Bogie.

98th Day

Bogie and I decided to drive into town today to Waitrose and get some more dog food and other provisions just in case this potential attack became a lockdown. We went in the Range Rover, Bogie driving, and I just sat in the passenger seat sipping coffee and enjoying the scenery of my home county until some bloody annoying oik cut us up in his rust bucket of a Ford Capri.

I told Bogie to blow his horn and make rude gestures at him while I smiled smugly through my passenger window, watching the rust bucket smoke into the distance.

I think our defences, now all in place, would see off the US Army, let alone Mr Hot Pants.

99th Day

I had another call from the chap who wears tight blue swimming trunks this morning.

He was asking how everything was progressing and that he would like to come and see me on his return from the south of France and come to the shareholders' meeting on the day of floatation. I replied, in the most confident manner I could, that this would be absolutely marvellous.

I was now becoming a little worried, even though I had guards with guns standing in every corner around the manor.

I told Bogie to order another rocket launcher.

100th Day

The new rocket launcher arrived today.

I love the way they wrap them up; it's not exactly Christmas paper but something not too dissimilar. The box is obviously large and very heavy and the deliveryman struggled lifting it out of his van.

I thanked him very much and took it into the house, nearly giving myself a hernia, and asked Bogie to sort it out.

They came with missiles, which was a godsend.

101st Day

I was worrying about Golden Mines floatation on the London Stock Exchange and the shareholders' meeting, which was supposedly going to now, I decided, take place on the 1 June. I was not sure how to handle the guy in the tight blue swimming trunks coming along to find out there was no one there and that Golden Mines did not actually exist.

I sat down in the kitchen with Bogie and asked him his advice while one of the guards was cleaning his machine gun at the kitchen table.

Bogie was practising loading the rocket launcher with missiles beside the Aga and he told me to stop worrying.

"Everything will be OK," he told me. "I will make sure of that, just leave it to me."

"Just to be even more sure," I added, "let's order a tank."

Bogie's face went into an instant grin, I'd never seen his eyes so wide with excitement.

102nd Day

The shareholders' meeting was taking place, I said to Hot Pants when he rang me this morning, at the Dorchester Hotel at seven-thirty on the morning of 1 June before the markets opened.

I explained that when the market opened and we announced that we had discovered gold big time the shares would rocket. As soon as the market opened his 50 million would soar five times within fifteen minutes, and I think he believed me.

The mine, according to the website, was situated in Kalgoorlie, Western Australia, and the Super Pit, we predicted, would produce up to 850,000 ounces of gold every year and its operation would therefore outweigh any other mining centre in Australia.

103rd Day

To be honest, when the morning of 1 June arrived I was not sure what I was going to do.

I was not going to be at the meeting and whatever room it was to be held in would be empty.

I would be here in the manor, protected by Bogie, my guards with their guns, and two rocket launchers and the tank.

Before I went to sleep tonight I poured myself a large whisky.

104th Day

I went to church again today and I got Bogie to drive me with the dogs. I'd had some strange dreams last night, which made me wake with a start several times.

Bogie didn't want to come in and while I listened to another very boring sermon he walked the dogs.

On my return from church to the Range Rover I slammed the door shut pleased to leave prayer behind me. Bogie told me he had been listening to the radio while waiting for me, Just a Minute, hosted by Nicholas Parsons, his eyes still streaming with laughter.

Herbert and Rusty were all over me, wagging their tails and covering me in dirt and licking my face with pink wet tongues.

I hope you don't think I'm trying to draw this story out. Recording my life with my pencil and notebook is comforting to me.

Mr Hot Pants is coming, and it is either his time or mine that might be coming to an end.

105th Day

Tomorrow was 1 June, the big day, and I had another phone call from Christopher Nelson as I was going to bed, who said jubilantly, he was looking forward to the shareholders' meeting at the Dorchester tomorrow and making a killing.

He told me he was at Nice Airport, just about to catch his flight, and would be at the Dorchester for the meeting at seven-thirty tomorrow morning, and that he couldn't wait.

I gulped at the other end of the phone and mumbled that I was looking forward to seeing him and told him that we would have to go out for a jolly good lunch afterwards.

I tried hard to sleep, but to no avail.

The security guards in the house did not help my night's rest, the floorboards creaking as they strode up and down the corridors of the manor. I could also hear the rumblings of the tank, which kept repositioning itself in front of the gate.

Herbert snuggled up to me extra close and Rusty, who had become quite fond of Bogie in my absence, never left his heels as he checked and rechecked the doors and windows, as well as shouting regularly at the guards to keep them on their toes.

106th Day

I awoke early, completely terrified.

I had already alerted the guards that today was the first day of something potentially dangerous happening.

I had the call, of course, from Hot Pants from the Dorchester at seven thirty-three am, who said he was going to kill me.

I tried to tell him to be reasonable but he was having nothing of that.

Apart from Mr Hot Pants' call nothing more frightening happened for the rest of the day, but we were all waiting for the trouble to begin. I hoped Bogie and I were ready and prepared for it when it did come.

Bogie had become very good at using the rocket launcher in no time at all, practicing as I had told him to on the swimming-pool house, which needed renovating anyway. He was trying to teach me how to use the other one but I was proving to be a bit dangerous using it.

It had one hell of a kick, and like my Purdey, bruised my shoulder.

107th Day

Today we just waited, looking out for big limousines and helicopters but nothing came.

Bogie was brilliant, instructing the security guys to keep on their guard.

We were as ready as we could be, and the manor was now like a fortress.

The guards paced about the place and Bogie spent the day cleaning his rocket launcher.

I don't know what I would do without Bogie and if we got through this I would give him a large bonus.

108th Day

And then it happened.

I jumped out of bed, downed my Scotch, while Bogie shouted at me to get dressed and come downstairs quickly. It was five o'clock in the morning.

I stumbled into my clothes, which I had arranged the night before, just in case, and then again stumbled, this time down the stairs, my heart racing, to appear in the hall where Bogie was standing looking at me, rocket launcher in hand, and saying, "Judge, trust me, we can do this!"

His eyes looked into mine in the most peculiar way. His look suddenly filled me with not only hope but courage and inspiration to win this battle. He then gave me a wink, so full of confidence, I felt I could follow him to the ends of the earth.

The dogs were barking incessantly and running all around us, also seeming to be looking for a fight.

I could hear the sound of limousines' doors slamming, machine-gun fire at the main gate, several explosions and the sound of roaring above getting louder and louder. Of course it must be the helicopter, no doubt with Hot Pants in.

I looked out of the front door to be dazzled by the searchlight on the helicopter shining down on us. It shone directly at me and Hot Pants must have seen my terrified face and my grey tangled hair being blown wildly about my head.

We had made a plan of course, after all it was all about protecting me. I wanted to protect everyone, especially Bogie and the dogs, but now was the time to be sensible and hide.

Bogie took me to the cellar and guided me down the stairs to sit surrounded by my huge collection of claret.

He left me there and ran back up the stairs, turning off the light and locking the door.

I could now hear gunshots and explosions and it sounded like the helicopter had landed.

So much for those rocket launchers; the attack had been too quick I suppose.

I could hear more gunfire coming from outside and then an enormous explosion – which I imagined meant Hot Pants and his henchmen had blown the front door in – and then the thunder of a small army.

The cellar door then burst open, the light switched on and Hot Pants was suddenly there, at the top of the stairs, looking down at me amongst my claret with his henchmen looking over his shoulders.

He did not look very happy; in fact he looked out of his mind. His face was so contorted with revenge that I could hardly recognise him. I wondered where Bogie was and hoped he was OK.

Christopher Nelson had a gun in his hand and he was pointing it at me. I was frightened but relieved he was not just dressed in his tight blue swimming trunks.

He walked down the cellar steps with his henchmen behind him, pointing the gun at me whilst I sat cowering on a stool.

They did not know, but beneath my stool was a trap door and once he had reached the cellar floor with his henchmen I pulled the latch and disappeared, like a magician's trick, under the floor in a cloud of dust and thankfully onto an array of mattresses and cushions arranged by Bogie the day before.

It was a reinforced bombproof concrete floor. I'd installed it at great expense to support my wine collection, which consisted of not only thousands of bottles of claret but also the best burgundies I had found on our many tours.

I could not see this but I hoped that Bogie would appear at the top of the cellar stairs – this was the plan – looking down at Hot Pants and his henchmen with the rocket launcher.

I knew he was there from deep below the cellar when I heard a huge explosion and guessed he had let off the rocket launcher at Hot Pants and his gang, who must have been no more.

Bogie always stood by me. Shame about my claret though.

We had some explaining to do to the neighbours.

They had, of course heard the explosions and called the police, so by about lunchtime my home was infested with dozens of police cars.

But there was not much evidence left. Bogie and the guards had been busy carrying all the dead bodies that lay on the lawn down to the paddock where, with the help of my digger, they created a mass grave.

Thank God for those rocket launchers, which were now hidden in the secret room below my non-existent wine cellar.

I simply explained in front of my bomb-struck manor to them that it must have been a gas explosion. I told them I had smelt gas for a few days now outside the laundry room, particularly while doing some cooking, but had thought no more about it.

They seemed to accept this and when they asked me what the helicopter was doing on the lawn, I said it was mine, and what business was it of theirs anyway.

Thank goodness they were not too interested in the broken-down front door and all the bullet holes and the front lawn not only looking well mown but cratered by landmines. I told them we had a problem with moles.

I was also surprised they were not more curious as to why there were so many security guards wandering around the place.

They seemed to be preoccupied, perhaps with some other investigation, and it was not long before all nine police cars paraded themselves, their blue lights flashing, out of the front gates.

109th Day

When I awoke this morning, it felt that all that had happened the day before must have been an incredibly bad dream until I struggled out of bed, pulled back my curtains, and gazed at my front lawn, the yucca upended, my oaks burned and broken, their strong branches now sliced to the ground and the tangled upturned lawnmower, which the woodcutter had left, after probably too much cider, in the middle of the lawn. It was half buried in earth and grass, no doubt as a result of a landmine or grenade explosion. Within the collection bin of the lawnmower, and covered in grass, I could just make out a decapitated head.

I closed the curtains, feeling a bit sick, and wandered downstairs in my dressing gown, sensing I'd had enough excitement in the last 24 hours to last me a lifetime.

I thanked the guards and gave them all a ten-pound note.

I then watched them climb into their three plain white vans and disappear slowly up the drive.

Bogie then appeared by my side and told me everything would be all right now and that he was proud of me.

I wiped a tear from my eye as the tank appeared from within the wood and turned out of the gate.

110th Day

Today I relaxed by the pool reading my book while the builders replaced the front door and all the gunshot windows as well as any brickwork that needed replacing or repairing on the manor's walls due to bullet holes. Bogie was busy repairing the lawns.

I couldn't help myself to a drink from the pool house, which of course lay destroyed and collapsed in a pile of rubble as a result of Bogie's rocket-launcher practice.

Bogie, however, just before lunch, brought me on a silver tray a glass of champagne and some cheddar sticks and told me to enjoy the sun while it lasted. He was going to oversee the reconstruction of my wine cellar and order lots more claret.

I was so pleased and grateful to him I decided at that moment I would adopt him as my son.

He would inherit everything.

111th Day

It was Sunday and decided I must to go to church.

I really did have a lot to be grateful for and wanted to say thank you.

112th Day

Now here's the bad news.

Mrs Jury had learnt of my good fortune and wanted half of it.

Now, divorce settlements can get very messy.

I know this from being a judge, but my experience of this gave me an edge, and even though Mrs Jury protested about my groping incident incessantly, I came out on top because of her incestuous behaviour.

I told her to settle out of court and I said I would give her £5 million and she was lucky to get that.

Before she switched off her phone I heard her say, "Where are my knickers?"

And then, as I had suspected, *"Oh ma bombe sexuelle, je pense que tu les as laissés dans la salle de bain."*

It was that French chappy, what a shit, and what a tart.

Good luck to him, she was definitely past her sell-by date.

113th Day

I said to Bogie, "Let's put the dogs into kennels and go on a cruise."

I told him I thought we deserved it and said I would pay, of course.

He was walking on air because I had given him a very large bonus of £50,000 and told him he was to be my heir. No wonder he was in a good mood.

For our cruise I went on the internet and explored the different options.

I went to cunard.co.uk and booked our tickets for a trip to New York from Southampton tomorrow.

The entire trip sounded absolutely splendid so I decided to use my new helicopter, which still sat on the lawn, to get to Southampton. All we needed was someone to fly it. So I telephoned the local flying school and arranged for a pilot to arrive at the manor early tomorrow morning.

114th Day

The pilot seemed a very nice chap.

Bogie and I put our bags in the luggage holder and jumped in and I hoped he knew what he was doing, as he took off in what seemed to me an extremely steep and hurried climb.

The early morning spectacle of what we call our green and pleasant land, as the sun rose, was spectacular.

We sped our way to Southampton, brushing cliff tops and church spires, sending cattle running. Starlings dusted the blue cloudy sky as if, with the many colours of a paint brush, we had painted a picture of an ocean of blue with a land of opportunity there before us. We knew where we were going.

The flight to Southampton Airport seemed to take no time at all and then we took a taxi to the boat.

115th Day

The website was absolutely right; we now find ourselves in the most marvellous place, where Bogie and I are having our every whim satisfied. The Queen Mary II is most certainly a lovely ship.

I loved standing on the deck with the fresh air engulfing me and watching all the beautiful people swimming and playing games. And the food was just fantastic. I didn't like the dancing though.

116th Day

There's only so much swimming you can do and the food was so lovely but there is only so much eating you can do. And being entertained by second-rate comedians, dancers and singers was getting on my nerves.

117th Day

Ship's chapel, more food and more swimming and more entertainment.

118th Day

After three days of luxury on this boat, I was getting very bored and wanted to get off.

And then I met this woman, a very rich American lady who was, she told me, the heiress to a cigarette company, and she constantly flashed her eyes at me.

A little older than I'm used to, but I saw another opportunity, and for her age, I had to admit, she didn't look too bad.

She was divorced and very available, I could tell.

She was also rather large, but I could deal with that.

Bogie was quite happy playing pool and chatting up pretty women and there were plenty of those.

119th Day

I asked this huge woman to have dinner with me. The Queen Mary II had the most exquisite dining rooms and she looked ready for it.

Her name was Rosemary Houston and she jumped at the chance and I treated her to roast duck and all the trimmings at a table with a wonderful white damask cloth with a candle on top.

She was very boring, but I was going to pursue this woman for her money. I would charm her and eventually, however repulsive, have to go to bed with her. After dinner I kissed her and then we both went to our separate cabins (thank goodness!).

120th Day

When I awoke this morning, I was not sure whether I could go through with this.

Although she was quite attractive in her own way facially, she had dreadful breath, and – as I have said before – was very big, enormous even, and both these things put me off.

But her wealth was worth going for.

I was relatively rich now and proud of it, some £125 million, but compared to her I was a fly.

Her wealth, which I had researched through Google, was estimated to be in the region $5 billion.

121st Day

I met her for breakfast this morning at nine o'clock on the forward deck. She seemed very keen to see me and smothered me with wet kisses.

It was a glorious day and the sea was rushing by, smelling of fresh and salty innocence, and an albatross was following the boat in elegant flight as we tucked into scrambled eggs with bacon and mushrooms and orange juice and coffee.

You would not believe how much she put away.

122nd Day

Today Rosemary Houston and I spent most of the day sunbathing together by the pool.

I think she is becoming quite fond of me, and she said when we got to New York she wanted me to come and stay in her mansion in Manhattan.

I must admit I felt a little nervous about this and thought I might have to use Bogie as an excuse to get me out of this situation.

Bogie was playing pool constantly and seemed to be becoming ever more popular with the girls on the boat as each day went by.

We were about to enter New York harbour and I was in two minds as to whether to pursue my new conquest or simply book a ticket for the return journey.

In the end, while gazing with awe at the New York skyline and the Statue of Liberty holding her torch so high, I plucked up my courage and reminded myself that, after all, this might well be another great opportunity to increase my fortune.

123rd Day

We had dinner at a restaurant called Quest on Broadway and then wandered back to her mansion, which was just around the corner.

It was a jolly nice restaurant and I had Butternut Squash Agnolotti with wilted kale and parmesan cheese and she had everything else.

I know I'm a bit chubby but she is huge and I can now see why.

124th Day

I managed to avoid her amorous advances last night but I knew my time was running out.

Today we were going to visit the New York Stock Exchange on Wall Street and watch her cigarette company's shares, she assured me, soar.

They did, because all over the news screens it was announced that her company, called Wellbeing, had acquired another – apparently undervalued – cigarette company, called White Smoke.

She was now worth another billion and although I could not bear the thought of sleeping with her I knew I would have to do so.

While I was going through this horrifying relationship, Bogie was living it up in a nightclub called Pacha and then spending most of the next day in bed at the Waldorf... I'd told him to relax and enjoy himself; he deserved to. I'd given him his large bonus as promised and also one of my credit cards while in New York to cover his expenses.

125th Day

I think the only course of action I had available was to try and marry this woman and live in New York.

It wasn't a bad place to live, I suppose, except for the bloody tall buildings, constant street noise of cars and car horns blowing, polluted air, pickpockets and street crime and an overabundance of fat people (I fitted in well!).

I reconsidered this last analysis of myself and concluded it to be unfair. To be honest I felt like a stick insect compared to this lot.

126th Day

My new objective of marrying this huge woman did not seem too difficult, as she seemed to adore me for some reason and because I still had some connections back in Old Blighty my divorce papers to the old Mrs Jury had arrived via email this morning. Perfect timing!

Things in this country do not take long to happen, so I asked her the question and she said yes immediately, so we set a date.

Tomorrow.

127th Day

This woman I was going to take on had enormous wealth, power and influence, so getting married at short notice in the most prestigious church in New York was absolutely no problem.

The church was called St Bartholomew's and overlooked Park Avenue.

Bogie was to be my best man and in future our butler and sleep in a room in the depths of the mansion and I told him he would have to smarten up but assured him he could still go clubbing occasionally.

Cafe St. Bart's at St. Bartholomew's Church meant you could have a church wedding and reception in the same place.

So after our "I dos", we moved to the 5000-square-foot terrace overlooking Park Avenue.

The new Mrs Jury opted for a pink wedding and looked absolutely huge in her large flowing pink wedding outfit.

There must have been a thousand people there. I felt overwhelmed, but that did not last long as I have never been made to feel so welcomed in all my life. New York's high society, these folks of the Big Apple, certainly knew how to party and we danced all night until the early hours, which suited me. The longer I could delay climbing into bed with this woman the better and with luck she might even pass out before we got there.

There was no prenuptial agreement so I knew I was quids in and certainly worth at least another billion, which made my wealth of some £125 million now seem irrelevant.

128th Day

I awoke with an enormous hangover and thank goodness I could not remember how we got home or much about the activities that took place in our bedroom the previous night.

The new Mrs Jury was lying on her back naked beside me, snoring. She took up most of the bed, leaving me with just a sliver to sleep on.

Her pink dress lay tangled on the bedroom carpet, along with a couple of empty bottles of champagne.

I crept out of bed and headed for the bathroom to find some Alka-Seltzer. I showered quickly and then crept quietly back into the bedroom to get dressed. After dressing I made for the bedroom door, intending to take a long walk and get some fresh air.

As I closed the bedroom door I heard a loud groan and then a shout of where do you think you're going?

I ran down the stairs as quickly as I could, told Bogie – who was watering the plants in the hall – that I'd see him later, and then out onto the busy street.

I'd made it, not only out of the house, to my relief, but had also made it big time. I was now incredibly wealthy so I punched the air and started to jog down the sidewalk, a large smile on my face.

129th Day

She announced we were going on a trip around New York.

She wanted to show me her city, with all those annoying tall buildings.

We ended up at the top of the Statue of Liberty; there was no lift and I don't know how we made it to the top.

130th Day

I decided I wanted to go to church so headed for St. Bartholomew's Church where we got married.

She remained in her mansion while Bogie was cooking her eggs – fried sunny side up – and sausages.

I was beginning to enjoy New York; the hustle and the bustle, those yellow taxis and even those tall buildings were beginning to grow on me.

131st Day

Today, I left the new Mrs Jury in her huge mansion eating roast beef prepared by Bogie, and decided to explore the Big Apple.

I took the subway and unfortunately got on the wrong train going the wrong way. As I travelled onwards the carriage became, at each stop, more full of young burly chaps wearing caps, tattoos and clutching baseball bats.

They did not seem to like the look of me and I was absolutely terrified.

In these situations you must keep your cool otherwise they will sense your fear and beat you up.

I managed to do this but not before they had stolen my wallet, my watch and the rings on my fingers.

132ⁿᵈ Day

Today I made sure I had the new Mrs Jury with me and Bogie when we went shopping.

We were heading for SAKS and I kept looking over my shoulder.

She bought most of the store and then we headed for lunch at Eleven Madison Avenue in one of those yellow taxis and the driver just never stopped talking.

Bogie rolled his eyes and, to be honest, I cannot remember what he was going on about apart from the fact he just loved the way I talked.

I spent the journey looking out of the window at the chaos going on all around us, while Mrs Jury took up most of the cab.

133ʳᵈ Day

Bogie was getting on very well as a butler, and this inspired Mrs Jury to hold a dinner party.

Many important and influential people came, speaking in the funny way they do, and I asked Bogie to arrange something typically English for them and I suggested bangers and mash with mushy peas and gravy.

When they arrived we offered them champagne, of course, and the men stood in fancy dinner jackets while the women sat in expensive dresses on expensive furniture in front of the fake fire in the drawing room.

They were all huge people.

All the guests seemed very interested in me, and I guided the conversation and amused them immensely, for what reason I do not know, but I enjoyed being the centre of attention.

When we sat down for dinner; this is when things went wrong.

They all enjoyed the bangers and mash and Bordeaux wines and Bogie was a brilliant waiter.

Then I just mentioned that I thought Americans were a little bit arrogant and seemed to think they could do anything and didn't know the geography of the rest of the world.

There was then a violent discussion resulting in our guests leaving, the last one slamming the front door very hard.

Mrs Jury was very upset and kept shouting at me until she was exhausted and then she went to bed. I decided to sleep downstairs on the sofa.

The entire evening turned out to be a complete disaster and I think I might have cost my new wife some friends.

134th Day

It was my birthday and Mrs Jury, despite my behaviour the previous evening, wanted to celebrate it.

So we headed off for another meal, this time at the Capital Grille, and then on to the theatre to see Jekyll and Hyde, a musical on Broadway.

I can't stand musicals but she insisted we go and she arranged a private box, several bottles of champagne and smoked salmon sandwiches so I could not complain.

Bogie remained at home. He'd asked me if it was OK if he entertained a girl he had met in the nightclub called Pacha. I told him, of course it was.

135th Day

We had a lunch party today and some different friends came because the ones we had for dinner the other night would not come.

These people, as far as I could see, laughed and laughed, without really laughing.

The lunch, because Mrs Jury told me to behave myself, went well, but I could not wait to get to the study, with my laptop, and check out all my friends on Facebook.

136th Day

Today, I went by myself to the top of the Empire State Building. I was not going to throw myself off or anything like that but I just needed to think. I was not totally happy with the new Mrs Jury and apart from the huge amount of money I had acquired from her she was making my life a misery.

When I got down to street level, I stumbled on a bar nearby called Legends and got hammered.

137th Day

I went to church again today, leaving Mrs Jury snoring in bed. It gave me more time to consider my situation and what I should do. Bogie had had enough of night clubs and had fallen out with his new girlfriend. And I had had enough of rich food and meeting the social elite of New York who, to be quite honest, bored me to death. Plus the fact Mrs Jury was too fat for me, slightly aggressive, and a complete pain in the arse.

138th Day

I awoke very early and climbed out of bed quietly so as not to disturb this whale lying beside me, and crept downstairs.

I thought it was time to return to the manor, so I checked the fights on my laptop and there were two last-minute seats available on a British Airways flight at nine o'clock from Terminal 7 at JFK.

I woke Bogie and told him we were going to make a run for it. He was all for it.

We closed the front door quietly and hailed a cab.

The flight from John F. Kennedy to Heathrow was without incident and at the earliest opportunity I ordered my double gin and tonic while Bogie had a lager. We watched a film and then slept on and off until our descent.

We took a taxi to the manor. I then dismissed the guard I had retained while we were away, and gave him a healthy tip.

It was good to be home again.

139th Day

Last night, I received endless calls from the new Mrs Jury, which I did not have the courage to answer. I eventually put my phone on silent and Bogie and I both went to bed early.

Feeling refreshed.

Sally had rescued the dogs from the kennels during our absence in New York and brought them over this morning. They rushed from her car and licked Bogie and me all over. It was great to see them again. We all enjoyed a coffee in the kitchen and then Sally had to go because she had a WI meeting in the village hall.

Bogie and I had a good day today: him doing some gardening, and me in my study, catching up on post and tons of paperwork.

One of the letters I came across was from a chap who worked on the Sunday Times Rich List.

He wished to interview me for an inclusion and I would apparently be ranked number 30, just behind a chap called Philip Green, who owned a few shops in London and lived a lot of the time in Monaco.

I said he could come and see me tomorrow morning if that suited.

I said come at eleven.

140th Day

He duly arrived on time and I showed him into my study while Bogie made us some coffee.

He was very impressed with my quickly amassed fortune and wanted to know more details as to how I had achieved this.

I asked Bogie to escort him to his car immediately and said goodbye.

141st Day

It was so good to be home but I did have a nasty feeling about the huge woman in New York.

I was trying to reassure myself, but this hung over my head and I just hoped she would be reasonable and let bygones be bygones.

What could she do to me anyway? She was so rich I thought she would probably put our relationship down to experience and look for her next victim, fingers crossed. Anyhow, the manor was now defended with electric fencing as well as my security gates. No guards, of course, but I didn't think I needed to worry.

After all, she would be looking for her next meal, not for me.

142nd Day

Bogie had a lie in and I went to church.

Again, another very boring service and on the way home I bought the Sunday newspapers.

When I got home I took a cup of coffee through to the drawing room to read them.

I remember sipping my cup of coffee as I opened the Sunday Times to see a picture of myself with the headline 'Groping Judge Amasses Suspicious Fortune'.

I unintentionally spat the coffee in my mouth onto my carpet.

This chap who had come to interview me on Friday had written the article and obviously had it in for me.

143rd Day

This morning there were a lot of press at the gate with cameras taking pictures of whatever they could.

I stayed indoors, closed the curtains and switched on the electric fence.

I told Bogie to go and tell them all to fuck off.

144th Day

Nothing had changed today and they were still there, snapping away at every opportunity.

I decided to ring this chap at the Sunday Times and have a go at him.

He told me I deserved the pain and I told him that even though I was a struck-off judge I would see him in court.

He laughed at me.

145th Day

They were still there this morning snapping away.

I could now see tents arranged outside the gate and they were cooking eggs, bacon and sausages on their portable barbeques.

Bogie asked me if I wanted him to get a pitchfork.

I said, why not? And take the dogs, they need some exercise. At this both Herbert and Rusty's ears pricked up, their tongues hung out and their tails started wagging.

When they saw Bogie and the dogs coming they picked up their stuff and made a run for it.

I thought they would probably be back though.

146th Day

In the morning, I saw a chap with binoculars peering over my wall.

I went – perhaps foolishly – to my gun cabinet, and retrieved my Purdey.

I called for Bogie and we both ran through the bushes until we could get a good view of him.

He was talking into his mobile and as we crouched below him behind the wall we could hear him saying, "I'm watching out for the pervert and I've got my camera ready."

I then arose from the ground and pointed my Purdey up his nose and he was gone.

147th Day

Another article appeared in the Times today, telling the story of how I was a pervert and groped women's bosoms and made my money from deceitful activities, saying basically that I had made my fortune by taking advantage of rich people by conning them out of their money. The article was headlined 'Fat Pervert's Road to Riches'.

This was scandalous and I decided I would sue the paper. Then I considered more carefully taking this action. I knew what they were saying was true, to some extent, but I did not want to help them advertise it.

148th Day

They did not seem to give up, and at regular intervals the press would pop their heads over the wall, snapping away with their cameras. I got used to it in the end.

The BBC rang me today to invite me onto Newsnight so that I could have the opportunity to defend myself, as they put it. I would have the chance to give my side of the story.

Newsnight followed the BBC News at Ten so it looked like I would have a double billing that night.

I said I would, because as a judge I knew how to put my case from my many experiences in court over the years.

I was booked for the Monday programme and they said they would send a car to collect me at four o'clock.

149th Day

Went to church today. Bogie drove and as the electric gates opened a mass of flashes came from the press and their cameras. Some kneeling, some standing, some leaning, hoping to catch the diamond, the picture that made me look like a paedophile, or a homosexual, or a murderer on the loose, or a grey old man with not much time to live, and, last but not least, the nation's most hated and detested person. Or more probably all of the above.

I hope you are having a good day.

I am getting to know the vicar and some of the congregation quite well now and they seem to have some sympathy for me, not much, but enough to let me leave the place and be able to live with myself.

My recent adventures made me imagine I was at the casino table with the croupier looking at me suspiciously. I was enjoying myself and I felt fulfilled, excited. I felt seventeen again, the age I'd started my legal studies, with all my life before me. I'd cast my dice and still had a massive pile of chips in front of me.

On our way home, I asked Bogie to stop the car and we picked some wild garlic from the verge.

I would do some cooking tonight, perhaps a chilli con carne, with some mince from the freezer.

150th Day

Another big day had arrived and, as they said, a BBC car with blacked-out windows arrived at the manor to pick me up at precisely four o'clock.

I didn't feel much like talking but when I did, to be polite, the driver completely ignored me. When he checked his rear-view mirror for up-and-coming traffic he did his best to look at me discreetly with total disgust.

When we arrived at BBC Broadcasting House in Portland Place my confidence was at an all-time low. I was rattled.

I had supper in their canteen surrounded by everyone you see on TV which was very odd. Instead of me watching them, they were all watching me now, and not in a friendly manner.

I was then hustled into the make-up room.

There was quite a bit of hanging around in what they call the green room but before I knew it I was sitting opposite someone who looked awfully like Jeremy Paxman.

The studio lights were extremely hot and I was sweating and the big cameras were moving around like Daleks all around me on a polished floor. *Exterminate, exterminate,* went through my mind, as they zoomed in on me.

I started to think I had made a big mistake.

He introduced me to the nation and then asked me his first question:

"Judge Jury, did you or did you not grope a woman's breast at the Guildhall?"

I fidgeted a little on my chair and tried to look relaxed in front of what was estimated to be, for this Newsnight they were calling A SPECIAL, 22 million viewers.

The cameras studied me like buzzards devouring a rancid piece of dead meat. I knew the lenses were zooming in on my sweaty face and Mr Paxman looked at me eagerly and impatiently, waiting for an answer.

He repeated his question.

"I say again: did you or did you not grope a woman's breast in the Guildhall?"

"Yes, but–" I eventually answered.

"So do you consider yourself a pervert?" he asked aggressively.

Another difficult question, I thought. I was impressed; he was obviously very good at this interviewing lark.

"Well, I suppose so," I replied, "but isn't everyone doing that sort of thing these days?"

From his expression I think I had flummoxed him.

"So, if that is true, which I don't believe for one minute, do you think it makes it acceptable?" he asked, trying to recover his ground.

I considered this carefully and for as long as I possibly dared. Even this Jeremy look-alike appeared anxious for a reply.

"Well, I suppose it does," I eventually said.

He looked even more flummoxed after this, and then after shuffling his papers, he asked me another question, looking like he knew something I didn't.

"I think we will leave that there now, but let me ask you another question. The American billionaire lady you courted on the Queen Mary II ocean liner and shortly after married, do you really think you are entitled to a billion dollars of her money?"

"Why not?" I said. "It's normally the other way round isn't it? The woman, in most cases I have witnessed, takes the man for all she can get."

I think he found that hard to argue with. He thanked me for coming into the studio and swivelled round in his chair to talk to the camera about something else.

I felt my appearance on the television had been a complete success.

A general election had been declared due to Labour losing a vote of confidence in the House of Commons and polling day would take place in four weeks' time.

So much for the summer recess.

151st Day

I slept well last night after the BBC car dropped me home. I was exhausted from the Newsnight interview but thought I could not have done more.

The newspapers today are singing my praises and instead of labelling me as a pervert they were now all declaring me a hero and a few even suggesting I stood for parliament.

I considered this at first with surprise and then, rubbing my chin, very seriously.

It was an easy decision in the end and I decided that I would, as a Tory of course.

I was now very rich and famous and I felt I must give something back to society and my country.

I walked with Bogie around the garden and I told him how beautiful it looked and asked him what he thought I should do. He gave me the nod while digging in a new shrub.

After this, I telephoned Conservative Central Office and they were pleased to hear from me.

They asked me to come and see them tomorrow at eleven o'clock and then to have lunch at the Carlton Club in St James's.

152nd Day

I arrived at 4 Matthew Parker Street on time and was welcomed with open arms.

They offered me the opportunity to stand for Brent North and I immediately told them to fuck off.

It was a safe Labour seat and there was no way I would get elected there. The only thing going for the constituency was that it housed Wembley Stadium and I loved football, even though I didn't know much about it.

And then I reconsidered. If I could pull this off I would be regarded as a potential future prime minister but I thought I better not get ahead of myself.

I accepted the challenge and then we were off to lunch, catching a cab with the paparazzi chasing after us on scooters.

Lunch at the Carlton was – as I had guessed – stuffy, with a public-school menu, but the claret was delicious.

153rd Day

Bogie presented me with breakfast this morning in the dining room and once again congratulated me on my nomination.

He was streetwise and coincidently grew up in Brent North and this would be invaluable to my campaign.

We would have to visit this hellhole though and meet all the dreadful people living there but I thought I'd put this off until tomorrow.

154th Day

The Labour MP who represented Brent North had a beard and had gone to public school, which I thought was a bit hypocritical, and probably opportunistic; him joining the party he thought would win at the time.

His name is Harry Stevenson and he had been a Member of Parliament for Brent North for sixteen years and I hoped the riff-raff who lived here might be sick of him by now.

Bogie and I trudged the litter-ridden streets of this dreadful place wearing our blue rosettes while people looked at us in disgust, but I was used to that.

I was pleased to have Bogie with me; he knew the area and if someone became violent he would deal with them.

I could not see the point of spending two hours each way sitting in traffic going back and forth to the manor, so I had arranged to stay in my usual room – plus one for Bogie – at the Ritz. After a day of abuse from the residents of Brent North I thought we both needed a little bit of luxury. Sally had kindly offered to look after the dogs.

155th Day

Our rooms are superb as usual and dinner last night was delicious, enjoyed with a very expensive claret.

We had a huge breakfast this morning and I felt ready and inspired to go back to Brent North to at least give this latest episode in this varied life of mine a try.

We took a taxi, and during the journey I took the opportunity to finish the speech I had begun writing last night. I was to address my conservative supporters in the town hall. I just hoped someone would turn up.

The place was packed, not only with conservative supporters but also with quite a few hecklers at the back.

I guessed they just wanted to have a look at me and get my autograph after my appearances on TV.

I don't believe in slagging people off like my Labour opponent, Harry Stevenson, so I began to talk about the future and how things can be better in Brent North and that I had many brilliant ideas.

I then went on to slag off Harry Stevenson in a big way and apart from a few shouts of 'pervert' that came from the back of the hall I finished my speech to huge applause.

Bogie was impressed and we both agreed my campaign was off to a good start.

156th Day

Both Bogie and I had a lie in this morning and I awoke to the sound of London traffic passing the Ritz far below.

I ordered breakfast in my room and read the Sunday papers while drinking strong coffee and sipping whiskey from my flask.

There was quite a lot of coverage of my speech yesterday in Brent North Town Hall and all of it was on the positive side.

To be honest the press were singing my praises and agreed with me that Harry Stevenson had held the seat far too long and that it was time for a change.

They said my speech had been inspirational and their opinion was that with a lot of hard work I had an outside chance of winning the seat.

They had interviewed several members of the audience who said that it was probably time for a change and one audience member said that she admired me baring my soul on the television over the groping incident and added that her husband did this all the time.

157th Day

This morning in the taxi to Brent North I had a call from the BBC.

They invited me to appear on Question Time this Thursday. It was taking place at Brent North Town Hall.

I said I would be delighted. I found this most satisfying and was chuffed.

158th Day

More touching of hands in Brent North and it was getting boring.

Bogie made the day though, by taking me to one of his old haunts where we enjoyed a smashing fry-up.

There was no sign of the Right Honourable Harry Stevenson and it seemed to me he was perhaps a slow starter and in my opinion a bit complacent.

I think he thought he was going to walk it.

159th Day

I think one of the aces in my pack was the fact I didn't have a beard.

There is an old saying that if you've got a beard you've got something to hide.

I had laid all my cards on the table: the groping incident and the receiving of a huge settlement from an American lady billionaire. I wondered what cards Harry Stevenson was holding close to his chest.

To help our cause, I asked Bogie to go underground in North Brent and find out more about him.

160th Day

While Bogie went underground I prepared myself for this evening's Question Time.

The BBC car collected me at six o'clock from the Ritz and took me to Brent North Town Hall.

I was put into make-up and we – by that I mean all the guests – sat waiting and drinking champagne in a back room until it was time to venture onto the stage and sit at the famous Question Time table.

There were five guests, as usual, and this was the first time I had met Harry Stevenson and we sat diagonally opposite, along with a comedian, an historian and another politician.

David Dimbleby was not there. He had been substituted instead by a lady, who looked like an antique dealer, was very attractive and wore lovely bright clothes. She had a husky voice and a long nose. When she looked for questions from the audience it looked like she was looking for the next bid.

She hinted about my groping incident and suggested that it was not perhaps my place to be an MP.

Harry Stevenson jumped at this and went into an enormous everlasting rant about how disgusting I was.

After he had been asked to stop ranting by the brilliant antique dealer, and this took some doing, I simply asked him one question, "Are you, Harry Stevenson, perfect?"

Guilt was painted all over the canvas of his face, more clouds and starlings, I thought.

He looked like a lamb bone waiting for a dog.

161st Day

I awoke early this morning in my suite in the Ritz and immediately felt pleased with myself. I had done reasonably well on the television last night.

I rolled out of bed, called for breakfast, and went to my bedroom door to retrieve my newspapers that lay on the corridor floor.

I then reclined on my pillows, having made myself a cup of tea, and rummaged through them.

Yes, there on the third page I was quoted, to my delight: "Are you perfect?"

There was a picture of Harry Stevenson leaving Brent North Town Hall looking sheepish and a picture of me smiling confidently getting into the black car with black windows.

Bogie called me; he told me he had some interesting information for me about Harry Stevenson.

162nd Day

Bogie told me something last night. Something I found difficult to believe, but it was a pleasure to hear it.

Apparently, Harry Stevenson, although a respectable MP, had a shadowy past.

I was delighted with the news, and I know I shouldn't at nine o'clock in the morning, and because I didn't fancy a scotch I reached for a wonderfully cooled bottle of champagne from the fridge and had a glass with my smoked salmon and scrambled eggs, which the porter – who looked like George Lazenby – had just delivered to my room.

163rd Day

I decided to go to church today to celebrate and I chose a little chapel in South Audley Street called Grosvenor Chapel, a beautiful place, but another boring sermon.

I had a drink in the Dorchester afterwards and a few people came up to me and asked for my autograph.

164th Day

What Bogie told me about Harry Stevenson, I found difficult to believe.

He had, apparently, been a male escort in his early twenties.

I told Bogie that we needed to find at least one woman who had spent the evening with this now pinstripe-suited pillar of society.

165th Day

It didn't take long for Bogie, who trailed the bars of Brent North, to find one woman now in her sixties, who had experienced Harry Stevenson's sexual ego and was prepared to explain how, in particular, he liked rough sex.

This was great news but I found myself pondering on how best to expose this potential election-winning scandal.

And then I knew what to do. I told Bogie to phone the shit at the Times who had written about me being the lowest of the low and tell him he had an exclusive if he changed his tune about me.

I was onto a winner and looking forward to destroying Harry Stevenson's career and becoming the new Member of Parliament for Brent North.

166th Day

When I awoke this morning, my head was clear.

I didn't feel hungry so the porter just brought me some coffee and the newspapers.

I sat in bed looking at the prints of Monet paintings that decorated my hotel bedroom and contemplating my election win.

But of course, there is always a twist, and things never come easy.

Harry Stevenson's voters were very loyal and liked his beard and felt him reliable and, even though he was now going to be revealed to be plainly an opportunist and sex maniac, it was often easier to stick with the devil you know.

My battle had not been won yet, but my bottle was full.

So I had another sip.

167th Day

Bogie's whisperings to that shit at the Times had done the trick and made front-page news.

HARRY STEVENSON, MP FOR BRENT NORTH, WAS A PIMP

I thought if that doesn't do the trick, nothing will. I must admit I felt a bit smug.

168th Day

So, I suppose, we now had two perverts to choose from: me or Harry Stevenson who denied the whole thing, saying he would continue to fight for his seat and that he intended to sue The Times.

Maybe, we were both equally qualified to take a seat in the House but I was determined to win. It was just a question of how I could put the cherry on top of the cake.

169th Day

I awoke this morning with what I thought was a brilliant idea to outsmart Harry Stevenson.

I jumped out of bed, showered and creamed myself up, checked out the details on Google, and then went down for breakfast in the restaurant.

I called Bogie and told him to join me.

Over fried eggs and bacon I explained my idea to him, which he thought was brilliant and I, of course, rang the press.

I like to go to church on a Sunday, as you know, and today I chose the Central Mosque Wembley on Ealing Road and made sure as many people as possible saw me entering.

What had dawned on me this morning, thanks to Google, was that over 17,500 people attended prayers on a weekly basis here.

Muslims turn to the mosque for help and advice for all matters in their day-to-day life.

The Central Mosque Wembley has trained *imams* to give religious advice and counsel on the many concerns of the community such as depression, youth challenges, cultural issues and marriage problems.

My groping issue was something they dealt with every day, I felt at home and they seemed to like me and at last I listened to a meaningful sermon.

As you can imagine my mind was going nineteen to the dozen; this simple conversion, I hoped, would deliver me many votes, not only from the Muslim community but, I hoped, from all.

170th Day

I have decided to become a Muslim and went to Waterstones, this morning, to buy the Koran.

I telephoned the Central Mosque Wembley and told them that I wished to convert to Islam although they told me that I was already a Muslim and had simply to revert. "Oh," I said, "OK."

The whole process was incredibly quick and easy.

Bogie fetched the Range Rover from the Ritz underground car park, drove me to the Central Mosque Wembley and all I had to say in front of two Muslims was, "I bear witness that there is no deity but Allah and I bear witness that Muhammad is His Messenger."

And that was that, all done.

I did not need to be circumcised, but was asked to take a basic course in Islam and visit Mecca at least once in my life time and pray five times a day.

They suggested I take a Muslim name so I opted for Hassan Judge Jury and I liked the ring of it. And I suppose, because they regarded me as an important person, they presented me with my robes, a graphite-blue Abbas thobe, and a green *kufi*. They let me change into my new clothes. I looked down at my dress and shoved my *kufi* to the back of my head. I looked good and I felt a billion dollars which, of course, I was.

I left the mosque with the paparazzi chasing me down the street to my parked Range Rover where Bogie stood cross-armed and ready to fend them off.

Tonight I decided not to shave. Like Harry Stevenson I was going to grow a beard. It would, of course, make me more popular. This must be why this Stevenson chappy had one, as well as everyone else in Brent North.

171st Day

It was not my intention to convert to Islam purely to get more votes, but because there was such a high percentage of Muslims in the constituency, I did not think it a bad idea. I thought it might show me to be an understanding and open-minded sort of chap.

I couldn't see what the huge difference was, one had the Bible, the other the Koran, one believed Jesus was the son of God, the other the messenger and both texts recall the life of

Jesus. I feel there is much misunderstanding on all sides when the overriding message coming from each religion is peace. Certainly nothing worth fighting about.

Just helped myself to another glass of scotch with ice. Although alcohol is considered haram (prohibited or sinful) by the majority of Muslims it was not going to stop me!

The whole of Brent North smells of curry. The delicious smell of cooking wafts from nearly every doorway and permeates the air of this place. Which suits both me and Bogie, we love a good curry.

This move of mine caught Harry Stevenson completely off guard and astonished, if not shocked him, and my own party thought I'd lost my mind.

I have decided to have a lazy day and read all about myself in the papers while relaxing in the Rivoli Bar sipping champagne in my new robes.

I was now a Muslim and I felt proud.

It is evening now and I'm in my hotel room in the Ritz. I have reached for another bottle from the fridge.

After taking my first sip, I put my glass down on my bedside table. I had an idea. I called Bogie and told him we were going out for a curry. The *imam* for Brent North had mentioned to me, in conversation the other day, that he was going out for dinner that night and after asking where he was going, he told me: Haweli of Ealing, you must try it, he said, it's the best place for a chicken tikka masala or choose whatever you fancy.

I showered, creamed up and both Bogie and I drove to Ealing to find out and we were not disappointed. We both enjoyed the Kingfishers, especially Bogie, and I was made to feel like a king by everyone eating there.

172nd Day

I was beginning, to be honest, to find this electioneering business rather exciting and with Bogie's encouragement I felt I could do this, yes really do this.

I now presented myself in robes befitting the religion I had adopted.

Everyone seemed to love it, and when encouraged, I would do a twirl after speaking in Brent North Town Hall.

The cheering I received could, I'm sure, be heard all the way to Westminster.

173rd Day

Just over a week to go now before the general election and the crowds coming to hear me seemed to be growing every day.

I don't think I was saying anything particularly interesting but my audience seemed to love the way I was saying it.

I stood before them in my robes; they were not worshiping me exactly but I felt they came close to it.

This was beginning to worry me.

174th Day

I didn't think I needed to do much more; my lead over Harry Stevenson was more than twenty-five percent.

I said to Bogie, let's go back to the manor for a couple of days and do some walking with the dogs. Thank goodness Sally had volunteered to look after them.

I thought they must be desperate to see us.

So this is what we did.

175th Day

As I guessed the dogs were all over us and Bogie and I went for a long walk in the sunshine, ending up in the pub.

The dogs enjoyed some water while Bogie and I sipped the local ale.

We opted to have lunch and tucked into bangers and mash and ordered two more beers.

The dogs were begging so I ordered them some sausages.

A few people came up to me and asked me for my autograph and I obliged.

The weather was becoming a little blustery so we finished up and took a long walk back to the manor, my robes blowing and rustling around my legs in the wind.

Bogie was giving me advice on the best way to handle the last week of my campaign.

Bogie always gave me good advice and I always listened, thought about it, and nine times out of ten acted on it.

He said, "Why don't you make a speech telling everyone that your conversion to Islam was because you believed in goodness for everyone?"

176th Day

Bogie dropped me off once more near the Central Mosque Wembley and in my robes I was looking for voters who I might convince to support me to be their elected Member of Parliament.

I wandered down the street with my new religion growing deeper in my heart and my new friends all rushing around me. Many shiny Mercedes rushed past, their electric windows down, and cheering faces leaning out with hoots of support. I felt humbled. Everyone around here drove a Mercedes.

It was a glorious summer's day and I felt good about myself; happier and more fulfilled than I have ever been in my lifetime.

People reached to shake my hand or even just touch me. The pavements were full of people from all creeds and cultures smiling at me. I felt a warmth come over me. I think it was love, an intense love.

Whatever it was it certainly did something for me. It got my heart racing and when it was time to leave I would always walk ten foot tall with a smile on my face.

And then this random person walked up to me on this glorious summer's day and shot me.

177th Day

I awoke in a white room in what I guessed was a hospital to find all sorts of tubes attached to me and oxygen fixed to my mouth and a beeping sound recording the beats of my heart.

Despite the gun wound, I didn't feel too bad.

The Northwick Park Hospital must have saved my life.

Bogie, of course, came to see me today.

He told me I had been very lucky and that none of my major organs had been penetrated.

I smiled at him and asked him to hold my hand.

I closed my eyes and prayed.

178th Day

One day to go until the general election, and I was lying in a hospital bed.

I was feeling better and the crazy drunkard who shot me was now detained.

Bogie came to see me again and told me I was now forty-five percent ahead in the polls.

That sort of lead had never been heard of before and of course it had something to do with someone trying to kill me and the sympathy vote, but I did not care, I just wanted to be an MP, now even more than ever.

I had another cause to fight for now, and this was for law and order and the protection of us guys, yes, you and me, who just go to work each day, love their children, and watch television.

It was the eve of the election and I left the Northwick Park Hospital through the revolving doors covered in robes and bandages.

The press had a field day dancing around me and I was blinded by the flashes from their cameras.

Bogie drove me back to the Ritz.

We switched on the television. The Conservatives were predicted to win a landslide.

179th Day

I did not need to do any more. I couldn't even if I'd wanted to.

I lay in bed recovering and watching the television with newspapers all around me and my face covered in Germolene and plasters.

The polling stations closed at 10 pm and Bogie was going to drive me to Brent North Town Hall to see the counting and meet the Returning Officer who would, hopefully, declare me as the new Member of Parliament for Brent North.

I was unsure whether I could pull myself out of bed to go, but I did.

When I entered the hall in my robes and bandages there was a round of applause, which I found very touching and, although painful, I raised my arms to thank them.

It was late into the night when we got the result and this obviously involved a lot of waiting around and having to talk to lots of very boring people, but when the result came, it was all worth it.

I had stuffed Harry Stevenson who had now lost the seat he had held for sixteen years.

Not just lost it, but lost it big time to a nearly assassinated Muslim and now newly elected MP.

180th Day

I was exhausted from the night before and so was Bogie, so I had told him to have a lie in.

Despite my exhaustion, I was up early with excited anticipation and waiting for the next part of my fantastic adventure.

I had the television on in my room and as the counting continued it looked like the Conservatives were heading for a majority of over 100 seats.

A week Tuesday, parliament would return and we would choose our speaker.

But I could not wait until then. I went down to the hotel lobby and as I left the lift people wanted to congratulate me and shake my hand.

The doorman opened the door for me and then showed me to a cab, where again he opened the door. I stuffed a twenty-pound note into his hand and I struggled onto the back seat wearing my robes and bandages.

"Westminster!" I declared.

I was so excited and wanted to discover my new place of work.

My new cause was burning within me: law and order and the protection of all my constituents whether Muslim, Christian, Hindu or those with no religion at all. All had played a part in electing me.

On my arrival, and to my complete astonishment, the policeman said I was not allowed to come into this place dressed like that.

I told him in no uncertain terms that I had been elected an MP dressed like this and so why shouldn't I?

But all you've got on are blankets insisted the policeman.

I tried to explain to him that my name was Hassan Judge Jury and these were not blankets, but robes.

To his credit, he did in the end make a telephone call and I was let in.

I wandered around, amazed as the architecture and the history of the place engulfed me. I was one of only 650, and felt proud.

I walked into the Chamber with its green seats and knelt before the mace to pray. It was a chance to get one of my five a day out of the way.

And then for fun, I walked, admittedly slowly and with some pain, up the 334 stone spiral steps to the top of the 153-year-old Elizabeth Tower to watch Big Ben strike the hour.

On my walk back down I stopped at one of the windows and gazed over London towards Brent North. I felt the responsibilities of my appointment weigh heavily upon my shoulders and I hoped I had the courage to deliver them.

181st Day

I left the Ritz this morning, Bogie driving, and went to the mosque and was greeted with affection.

Now I was a Member of Parliament they wanted me to do all sorts of things for them, but I suppose, that's constituents for you.

And then my mobile rang. It was the prime minister. He asked me to visit him at Downing Street tomorrow at eleven o'clock.

I wondered, what had I done wrong?

182nd Day

I walked up Downing Street in my robes with the cameras flashing and people cheering and then walked through the black door.

I was shown through to the cabinet room, I knew it was the cabinet room because it was written on the door.

He leapt up from behind the huge table and strode forward to greet me with an outstretched hand.

He told me that my result at Brent North was astonishing and that he would like me to be his new Home Secretary.

"Dressed like this?" I asked him.

"I don't care how you dress; I think you've got the soul for the job."

I had done nothing wrong after all, in fact the complete opposite, and I was totally astonished.

183rd Day

It was a bit of a waiting game now; parliament returned on the 1st of September. I decided Bogie and I would take a weekend break after our hard work and disappear under the radar for a sort of retreat in Malta. I needed to steady my nerves.

And I was, after all, recovering from a gunshot wound and was meant to be convalescing.

I deserved it; after all, I'd won a Labour stronghold, become a Muslim, been shot and now I'd been asked to be Home Secretary.

I needed a little break before my work began.

184th Day

Our touchdown at Malta Airport was spotless.

It was jolly hot so I had to take all my robes off. I put on my shorts and a sleeveless top.

Both Bogie and I were pleased to be here and I was grateful for the chance to switch off from all the attention forced upon me in England.

After lunch at the hotel we decided to hire a little boat and go fishing; we found it easy and we caught lots of bream.

Neither of us had ever done this before, beginners luck, I think, a bit like my political career.

I suppose there must be similarities between fishing, religion and politics.

We then went swimming. I'd bought a pair of bright blue swimming trunks, just like Christopher Nelson's, at Gatwick airport. The water was crystal clear and, afterwards, we returned to our hotel, the Victoria, feeling refreshed.

185th Day

I found a beautiful church in Old Bakery Street this morning, while Bogie snored away, called St Augustine. I took the opportunity of doing one of my five of the day and had a moment of prayer.

It was a bit of a walk but I needed the exercise and the smells of the sea and the cooking and the sight of women hanging out their washing high above the cobbled streets and the colours made me feel very lucky to be here. In fact it made me feel happy and thankful to be alive.

Yes, my duties as Home Secretary were uppermost in my mind but this short break was doing me good and had given me renewed energy to fulfil it.

Home Secretary. I still can't believe it!

We flew back this evening and took our usual rooms in the Ritz.

Tomorrow parliament returns and we, the MPs, were going to choose the speaker of the House of Commons.

186th Day

I had to swear my oath of allegiance today, which I was quite happy to do.

I held the Koran in my hand and stood there in my robes surrounded by respectable men in suits.

In the afternoon I had another meeting with the PM and he guided me through my future duties as Home Secretary.

I was determined to sort out law and order and he was right behind me.

Afterwards I returned to the Ritz and joined Bogie for a splendid dinner.

He had spent the day running around London in a tracksuit I had bought him from Lillywhites.

187ᵗʰ Day

I had lots of papers to read, which arrived this morning in a red dispatch case delivered by a dispatch rider to my room.

As Home Secretary I was not given a grand gaff in Downing Street like the PM and the Foreign Secretary so I was still hanging out here at the Ritz, which I didn't mind one bit and neither did Bogie.

I was filled with horror by how many papers I was expected to study and it did not take me long before I stuffed them unread back into the case, shut it, finished my Scotch and went for a walk along Piccadilly.

I had better things to do.

I walked towards Piccadilly Circus through crowds of people who just wanted to touch me, and arrived beside Cupid, his bow and arrow and the waterfall.

And then this woman came to my side and told me she wanted to be my wife.

She told me her name was Samantha Clark and that her father had been an MP in the 1970s and the late 1990s, had written many diaries and loved classic cars and had died some years ago.

I think Cupid had done his job and I fell in love with her immediately.

I took her back to the Ritz to have some tea, which was followed by dinner.

After dinner I gave her a kiss on the cheek and opened the door to her taxi and she went home to Chelsea.

188ᵗʰ Day

This morning I opened the red case again. I knew I must tackle this paperwork and put together my proposals for this new parliament before the Queen's speech in five days' time.

I know the devil is in the detail but I felt spending too much time wading through endless pieces of paper would result in me losing my way in what I considered the key objectives I should achieve as Home Secretary.

With these objectives in mind I began preparing my maiden speech.

Enough for one day. I called Samantha and told her that I was too tired to do anything this evening and was going to bed with a tray of cottage pie and a good claret. She understood.

189th Day

As well as listing my objectives last night, I did manage to struggle my way through that paperwork in my dispatch case this morning and then I telephoned Samantha and suggested we meet for lunch at Cecconi's in Burlington Gardens at noon.

I was collected by the ministerial car at nine and taken to the Home Office, where I met my team of civil servants. I gave them an inspirational speech, to which they gave me loud applause and lots of cheering.

And then I left to get into my ministerial car with my government aide congratulating me whilst walking by my side. Before I got into the back of the car I said to my government aide, sack them all. He looked flummoxed but bowed his head.

When I arrived a little late at Cecconi's Samantha was at the bar sipping a glass of champagne. I guided her to a table I had reserved in the corner by the window.

The waiter brought me a glass of champagne and we sat in silence for a while, gazing out of the window looking at the people walking by, she dressed in Chanel and me in my robes.

After people had stopped asking for my autograph, I ordered for both of us: crab ravioli and beef tomatoes and basil.

We enjoyed a bottle of perfectly chilled Cervaro and she told me more about herself.

A journalist, the daughter of a famous and much loved MP and diarist and she still owned one of his classic cars, a Jaguar

XK120, and a Rolex Daytona, which lay heavy on her wrist, and several Degas paintings.

She told me of her days growing up in Kent and I could see in her eyes how much she missed him.

She clutched her glass and smiled fondly at me, saying I reminded her of him.

190th Day

Both Samantha and I went to the mosque in Brent North early this morning.

I explained that this was something I had to do. I told her to get used to people touching her and cheering, this is what they like to do. They seem to really like me and they will love you. It's affection I explained.

When we got back to the Ritz we changed into our running kits and went for a run around Green Park, my parliamentary papers and my proposals complete.

After this we both had a shower and I creamed myself up.

I met the prime minister this afternoon. He was hesitant about my proposed policies but I convinced him to be radical and to be possibly the greatest and most memorable prime minister since Robert Peel.

He liked the comparison.

191st Day

The state opening of parliament was an enormously pompous affair. I had seen it on television, of course, but to actually be there, squeezed together like sardines in a sardine tin, my nose pressed up against the back of the prime minister's healthy head of hair – which smelt, believe it or not, of sardines – was surreal.

And then, after Black Rod had tried to break the door down, we had to walk through the Central Lobby to the House of Lords with our shadow opposition members walking beside us. The Shadow Home Secretary who walked with me turned out to be a jolly nice chap. He had been the previous home secretary when labour were in power. We had a bit of a laugh because he told me how much he liked my robes and that when he was able to let his hair down he liked dressing up in women's clothing. I told him I enjoyed doing the same but always felt a tinge of vulnerability.

To be so close to the Queen and hear her speak sent shivers down my spine. And when she spoke of her government's intentions, some of which were my own, I knew in that moment, if ever I had to lay down my life for her and our country, I would do so.

192nd Day

When I stood to make my maiden speech, I rose from my seat beside the prime minister, gathered my robes around me, and then waited for silence.

Then I said, "Listen, watch and learn." There were a few snorts from the opposition benches and then I was off.

"Have any of you dressed in women's clothes for a day?" I asked, looking towards the shadow home secretary, who smiled approvingly at me. "You should all try it, you will feel vulnerable and hunted."

The House of Commons fell silent and you would have been able to hear a pin drop. My stern gaze rested on the respectable men all around me.

"As Home Secretary," I said, "I will introduce a national cross-dressing day to be held on Valentine's Day each year. A greater respect will be shown towards each other.

"And I intend to bring back hanging. I've been labelled a pervert in my past and I know both sides of the coin, so don't get me wrong; when I say something it is after much consideration."

I looked about the House and saw open-mouthed faces. After years of slanging matches, for once the benches remained quiet.

The speaker looked at me, encouraging me to go on, and the House remained silent, waiting in anticipation.

"I will put more bobbies on the beat, and when I say more, I mean fifty percent more. I have discussed this with my right honourable friend, the prime minister and he is as determined as I am regarding this matter."

I turned to look at the prime minister and he was nodding his head in agreement. "So we intend to double the police budget. This will make a difference, I promise you, and they will have a lot to do, they will be busy.

"And because they will be busy working to protect our people from the scum of our land they will all be paid more. I intend to implement salary increases for the men and women of our great police forces. I will start with an immediate salary increase of twenty-five percent followed annually by a five percent increase thereafter."

The House was listening and I looked about me, my robes wrapped around me, and my head held high.

"I will also use this opportunity," I said, looking around the chamber, "to radically change the makeup of our police force. Efforts have and are being made in this direction but with my example of welcoming all men and women from all religions and any colour I intend to see bobbies, both Muslims and Christians walking together side by side. And walking together we will rid our streets of criminal gangs, knife gangs and hard drugs."

I was beginning to get a response from the House now and I could hear rumblings like, hear, hear! and wharf wharf and cheering and then even a little clapping.

"I will take Canada's lead and legalise marijuana." This made quite a few members start coughing but I felt I still had them with me. "Legalising marijuana," I continued, "which I have certainly smoked, and probably all of you too, will diminish the drug gangs' revenue and make easier the difficult job of our police force."

The house was now warming up and even the opposition benches were nodding in agreement and uttering reluctant, hear, hears.

"I will," I continued, "welcome illegal immigrants entering our country under lorries, they have, after all, in desperation and with much courage made it to our shores travelling thousands of miles. These people will find work and a new home and will contribute enormously to our economy and our national health service as well as in many other ways.

"I will put an end to Chinese and Russian billionaires buying multi-million-pound houses in London they never live in, while our countrymen sleep on the streets. We will rid our streets of homeless folk and our churches of all faiths all around our nation will open their doors to them and with government support feed them, clothe them and keep them warm in winter. And get them prepared for work, yes to work hard, as we must, as we all must, to make our economy great once more."

The entire house burst into applause and it took the speaker more than ten minutes to bring the house to order.

"And there is more, for a start: litter, chewing gum and, of course plastic! Hefty fines and community service for the culprits." I took a sip of the whisky I had arranged to be placed by the dispatch box.

I paused and wiped my mouth with my handkerchief, looking around the entire House, making sure everyone was paying attention to my every word.

"Yobbish and threatening behaviour," I continued, "I have already put into place a request for the installation of several rows of stocks to be placed on the grass of Westminster Square, along with large buckets of rancid fish and meat and vegetables, ready for the public to toss at the scum of our communities.

"My policies are based on zero tolerance," I continued in a whispering voice, "and our nation needs them now more than at any other time. And just one more thing, we must never be ashamed of ourselves here in this House. We all work tirelessly for our country and we will all have to do more, much more, because our people do not appreciate that yet and we must convince them."

Remembering Bogie's words, I added, "I believe in goodness for everyone as I'm sure you all do."

I finished by encouraging all in the House to use their privilege to do amazing things.

With that I presented my finale by dropping my robes to the floor and standing in front of the entire House of Commons in my tight blue swimming trunks. I couldn't help myself and did it in memory of Christopher Nelson, who was now pushing up daisies.

The House, after a unified sharp intake of breath, looked completely stunned.

My ministerial car dropped me back at the Ritz and before I went in I picked up a copy of the Evening Standard from Harry, the man who gave them away just outside the doors of the hotel. I asked him if he'd had a good day and he said yes apart from some yob spitting in his face for no reason at all. I told him we were going to do something about that and then entered a world he could not even imagine: the Ritz.

Samantha and I had dinner in the hotel tonight, a lovely dinner, and she didn't take her eyes off me all night. And yes I believe it is probably the most beautiful dining room in the world.

Bogie had gone home to do some gardening and look after the manor and the dogs.

We are in bed and I've just had a call from New York, it was good news, the annulment of my marriage to Rosemary Houston had just come through. I told Samantha and we did a high-five.

193rd Day

The morning papers were covered in colourful pictures of me standing in the House of Commons wearing only my tight blue swimming trunks.

After breakfast I took Samantha to do some shopping. But first I took her by the hand to the Royal Academy to meet David Hockney.

I'd been flabbergasted to receive an early-morning call from him which had been put through to my hotel room. He asked if I would like to have a look at his pictures and that he would like to personally show me each one and tell me stories of his time in California.

He greeted us with a broad smile, dressed flamboyantly and sporting a wide-brimmed hat and smelling of cigarettes. He congratulated me on my maiden speech and spent an hour of his time showing us his beautiful works of art. I was a big fan. When it came to saying our goodbyes he nearly knocked me off my feet when he asked if he could paint a picture of me in my tight blue swimming trunks in front of one of his famous swimming pools. Well, I was speechless and Samantha saved the day by saying of course he could. He was very pleased and explained I would not have to do any photo shoots as he could work from the many pictures of me on the front pages of the newspapers.

Samantha and I left the Royal Academy ecstatic and made our way to the Burlington Arcade. I wished to buy her something special. We stopped outside Richard Ogden Jewellers and she pointed at a ring and I bought it for her and then I proposed and she said yes so we went to Le Caprice, where I carefully took the ring out of its blue box and put it on the third finger of her left hand. Diamonds glittered in the candlelight and she asked when and I said tomorrow.

194th Day

We got married today in the Grosvenor Chapel in South Audley Street. Bogie, whom I'd told to stop gardening at the manor and bring the dogs, was my best man once more.

So it was just Samantha, me, Bogie and the dogs and the priest, who is called Mary, blessed us all. She is as liberal in her thinking as I am and the fact that I was a Muslim did not seem to bother her at all.

After the service we walked down South Audley Street together – Bogie scattering confetti all over us and the dogs tugging at their leads – to the Dorchester where I had my hair and beard trimmed before having a delicious lunch of roast beef while surrounded by leather and marble, the restaurant staff allowing Herbert and Rusty to lie at our feet.

While Samantha and I drank a delicious claret, Bogie drank numerous pints of lager and became a bit too amorous towards Samantha so I told him to go home and sober up.

He left the restaurant for Paddington with Herbert and Rusty and then Samantha and I enjoyed some pudding.

Afterwards Samantha drove us back very quickly to the Ritz in her Jaguar XK120. We laughed all the way and once we got to my room she pulled the robes off my shoulders and we fell into bed.

195th Day

I'd been neglecting my friends on Facebook and couldn't remember when I was last on it; it must have been yonks ago. I'd noticed a lot of notifications and friend requests coming through but had not had the inclination to look any further.

I pushed the red dispatch case, once again stuffed with papers, away from me to the side of the table in my room at the Ritz and decided to see what was going on. Samantha had left early and had gone to work at the Daily Telegraph.

I tapped the Facebook icon on my iPhone.

To my astonishment I had a Facebook memory showing a picture of me and my original Mrs Jury enjoying ourselves in the Dordogne with that slippery French chappy hovering in the background, a death threat from the huge American woman in New York, and over twenty-five million friend requests and climbing by the second.

Impulsively, I decided to accept them all straight away and within seconds I had hundreds of messages flooding through in front of me. Their profile pictures came from all over the world.

I carefully worked my way through them. Apart from a few, who admitted they were sex perverts too and hero worshipped me, most of the messages I received wanted – or rather were begging me – to do just one thing.

With this social-media stuff, I guessed I'd gone global.

I was chuffed, more than chuffed to be honest.

I lifted my whiskey glass to my lips.

196th Day

After excitedly discussing with Samantha last night, what was not a dilemma to me because I knew what I was going to do, I called the prime minister this morning and told him I wished to do something completely different.

I resigned as Home Secretary and gave up my seat as Member of Parliament for Brent North. What a relief.

I could hear him choking, at the other end of the line, on what I thought must be his sandwich. "But – " I heard him say, and then I put down the phone.

I'd tried to do my bit, but politics was behind me now. The new government policies I have put in place would, I hope with a fair wind and for our nation's sake, become Acts of Parliament.

I now had something much more important to do, and according to my Facebook friends I was the only person in the world who had any chance of doing it. I felt euphoric and Samantha was excited; she was looking forward to a change.

197th Day

The Saudi Arabia football team wanted me to be their new manager and so did – now and counting – thirty-six million Facebook followers.

With ministerial cars not coming to get me anymore and no more red boxes stuffed with ministerial papers haunting me, I slept like a baby last night.

I jumped out of bed this morning, put on my trainers and ran three times around Green Park, Samantha trying to keep up with me.

I looked at myself in the mirror after I had showered and creamed up and I didn't recognise myself. Who was this slim, not overly muscled, good-looking guy, looking back at me?

Samantha then came out of the bathroom and jumped onto the bed and started jumping up and down with excitement.

198th Day

We landed at King Khalid International Airport and were welcomed in Arrivals with open arms by the Saudi King and their nation's international football team, who looked at me hopefully as if I could perform a miracle.

And this miracle, if it was going to happen, would have to take place in two months, three days, four hours, forty-nine minutes and ten seconds. I was looking at the large clock on the wall above the exit doors.

The heat was just unbearable. I thought it was hot in Malta and Morocco but this place was like an oven. It felt, as we emerged from the airport, like I'd walked into a sauna. *This is what you call hot*, I thought, pulling at my robes. I'd go to the best tailor here and get decked out like these guys in white incredibly thin silk and an *agal*, a band round my head and a *keffiyeh*.

Everyone here kept bowing at each other and I found myself doing the same, it was infectious.

No wonder they were no good at football. You can't play football in this heat so perhaps this was the problem. Or perhaps this was the solution! Our chaps from home would find this climate exhausting to play in and so would the Germans, so this could help with our chances.

The heat was frazzling the hair in my nose and my head felt like it might explode. I threw my *kufi* and robes into the first bin I saw after I'd got out of my huge white air-conditioned car and ran for the air-conditioned hotel lobby – where everyone was playing backgammon in white silk – as fast as I could, wearing only my bright blue swimming trunks.

I rushed for the lift, Samantha holding my hand, and as the doors were closing I looked back into the lobby of the Ritz Carlton. They'd paused their games and were, their necks strained, looking at me.

I had arrived.

The World Cup was taking place, just down the road, in Qatar. It was jolly hot there too.

199th Day

Samantha and I had an early night last evening after a totally disgusting meal of goats' eyes and chips in our hotel restaurant. I could see people from England spending money they didn't have, on silver, yellow and blue cards.

I left Samantha to enjoy the pool and pamper herself and set off.

Today I was going to find the best tailor in Riyadh. I needed some clothes that kept me cool.

I was getting into the habit of running from one air-conditioned building to another while Samantha lay by the pool.

Looking for a tailor here was easy. I was a very important person: the manager of the national football team, and all I wished for I could have. It is incredible how gentle and lovely these people really are.

Yousef, the doorman at our hotel, said, handing me a piece of paper with some scribbling on it, this is where you should go for your clothes: Al Harithy. And then jokingly he added, they know how to stitch you up!

I arrived at this Al Harithy place in my white air-conditioned limousine with blacked-out windows and then asked the driver, who'd introduced himself as Boulos and who'd not stopped talking all the way, to open my door and I stepped onto the pavement, which looked like it was about to melt, and accelerated to the shop's front door and into the tailor's air-conditioning.

I had my Saudi Arabia Football Team tracksuit on, and trainers.

There were lots of dogs here, and cats eyed you from every corner. They looked like they didn't like the heat here either and only had odd patches of fur, the rest scratched off, I guessed, trying to get rid of the fleas.

Once in this place of gentlemen they took me to the back room and stroked me all over with measuring tapes and then gave me a coffee.

Pictures of Saudi princes covered the walls and there was a picture of the Queen with Roger Moore standing beside her in front of Windsor Castle.

I asked, whilst flipping through a copy of *Vogue*, one of the tailors when it would be ready and he told me, to my surprise, "by the time you finish your coffee."

200th Day

So, this morning, we were at the King Fahd International Stadium early before it got too hot.

I'd sent the team a message last night before I'd gone to sleep: seven o'clock and don't be late or you'll all be sacked.

They were all there, looking anxious to please, sweating and dressed in their green and white football kit. I did wonder why they had been so keen to have me as their manager. Was it the power of social media, which above all described me as a motivator who achieved great things? The fact I knew nothing about football did not seem important to them.

"Now," I said, in a very loud voice, "start running! Up and down the pitch rolling your arms at the same time in clockwise and anticlockwise motions with your heads looking at the sky."

"Now, do it!"

I made them do this for two hours until they were exhausted. After this the captain asked me why I was not asking them to do some football training. I told him this *was* football training and he shook his head, not understanding.

But I knew from my years in law that if people arrived to talk to you about something it was better to talk about something completely different. I had decided, deliberately, to apply this technique to their football training and I hoped they'd understand.

As I dismissed them all to the showers I said take one of these and I placed a white envelope in each of their hands.

They did not know yet, but inside each envelope was an airline ticket to Geneva and two weeks skiing in Zermatt, staying at the Grand Hotel Zermatterhof. I could afford it and

I thought two weeks' skiing in a place where the temperature was a bit cooler would be the ideal incentive.

I stood outside the changing rooms listening to them all talking excitedly and wondered whether this enormous challenge could ever be fulfilled. And then I heard this loud cheer from the shower rooms.

They must have opened the white envelopes.

After I'd got back to the Ritz Carlton driven by Boulos and after I had kissed and cuddled Samantha I called Bogie to see if the dogs were OK and if all was well at the manor.

He said it was all cool there.

I was jealous.

201ˢᵗ Day

This morning Samantha and I made love before sunrise.

She'd been fidgeting all night and could not sleep, and eventually admitted to me, under the sheets with a mischievous smile and a twinkle in her eyes, she was feeling horny.

After that we showered and I creamed up and then we visited Mecca, the birthplace of Mohammed, as I had vowed to do once in my lifetime when I became a Muslim.

Being here made it easy; it was only down the road, and if I wished I could visit the place once a week. We were driven in the large white limousine by my personally appointed chauffeur, Boulos.

In the afternoon I left Samantha at the hotel and was driven once more to the training ground at The King Fahd International Stadium, also nicknamed the Pearl by my chauffeur, who I was getting to know quite well. He was a good chap and very helpful explaining much about his beloved country and was extremely excited and enthusiastic about being appointed my personal driver and he never stopped talking. He told me that in his lifetime, he had been a pilot for the Royal Saudi Air Force and had taken part in the first Gulf war and that when he left the air force he worked for the Saudi Telecom Company until he retired. For a little extra income in his retirement he had chosen the profession of chauffeur. He was married for some 35 years now and had two grown-up children. And his passion, like most Saudis, was for football.

He knew the names of the whole Saudi team and gave me endless advice on what strategy I should take to improve the team's game. He told me the names of some players he thought should be in the squad and the names of those in the squad he thought should not. He told me he would switch the players round. He thought half the team were playing in the wrong positions. His enthusiasm was infectious but as I knew nothing about football he'd lost me several times.

On our journey through Riyadh we passed endless rows of palm trees dwarfed by skyscrapers, some of which I recognised such as the Kingdom Centre, with a sky bridge connecting two towers, and the *Al Faisaliah* Centre, with a glass-globe summit. Both structures disappeared into the intense blue cloudless sky. And all around this city, which sat on a plateau, sand dunes went on forever and ever to meet the skyline.

With Boulos talking nineteen to the dozen, and not really understanding what he was saying, my mind began to wander and I drifted into another world.

As I was gazing out of the car window looking into the distance, his voice became a gentle hum.

I was feeling tired, probably from my morning activities with Samantha and our visit to Mecca, which had involved a lot of walking.

In the distance I saw what must have been a mirage: an oasis with water, palm trees and sand. On this island I could see my football team with scarabs, dismembering both of my previous Mrs Jurys and chucking their body parts into the water. I awoke with a start and told Boulos I needed a drink.

You were not meant to drink here but Boulos obliged, with a wide grin on his face in the rear-view mirror, pressing a button beside his steering wheel, after which a drinks cabinet appeared in front of me in the back of the limousine.

I helped myself to a large gin and tonic with plenty of ice.

Thank you Boulos, I said and took a large gulp. I think, since I became a Muslim, I have become a better person, more understanding and certainly less arrogant. But I wasn't going to stop drinking. I took another large gulp, then lifted my glass to Boulos, who was smiling at me in his rear-view mirror, and said cheers.

He then said to me laughing, "Let's hope for many of them when we, The Falcons, who we, in our country call Al-Saqour, win the World Cup." The Saudi Arabian football team were known as the Falcons. Boulos went on to tell me how excited his country was that I had come to be their manager. After which he sang to me what must have been a happy-sounding native song, all the way to the stadium.

Then we arrived at the ground and Boulos jumped out of the car and opened my door for me. I stepped out of the air-conditioning and into the heat and he bowed to me and I bowed to him.

Then I had a thought. I said to Boulos, leave the car here and come with me. I want you to give the team a pep talk. He was, at last, lost for words, until I reassured him and then in an instant his ever-constant smile returned to his golden unshaven face; his confidence had returned. His ocean-blue eyes looked at me for help in this task.

I told him not to worry and to just shout at them as loudly as he could – that would strike fear into their hearts – and then tell them why they are the greatest nation on this earth.

Tell them the history of your country, I said, like you've told me. Tell them exactly what you think is wrong with their game and how you would go about improving it. Tell them they can do better and can be champions of the world. I think you know what to say, I said, and I think you can do it far better than me.

His face was a picture of all his ancestors all rolled into one.

"Will you come with me?" I asked.

After a pause he lifted his head, looked me in the eyes and said, "Yes I will." He then kissed me on both cheeks and said, "*Shukran jazilan.*"

We left the huge white limousine with blacked-out windows shimmering in the car park and together we walked into the stadium.

When I got back to the hotel this evening Samantha was asleep. I crept quietly into bed with her and listened to her gently breathing, the words of Boulos speaking to my team this afternoon going round and round in my head.

202ⁿᵈ Day

Over breakfast with Samantha, I told her all about Boulos' impressive step onto the world's international football stage.

I told her, over our figs and *shakshuka*, which is basically their version of scrambled eggs, homemade jams and hummus, and the most beautifully home-baked bread and rich dark coffee, about our training session yesterday.

I told her that when we arrived at the training ground the captain immediately came up to me, begging for his team to play some football. We need to play football, he told me, if we have any chance of qualifying for the World Cup! I told him to sit down and be obedient.

He then stood up again and continued to spout off, saying, "But Grand Mufti [that's what he called me], we have to practice, we can't just run up and down the pitch waving our arms around, we must pass to each other and score goals." He could see he was getting nowhere with me and so sat down, exasperated, on the bench in the dressing room and put his sweating head in his hands.

I then introduced Boulos, who was standing behind me. You can do this Boulos, I whispered to him, as he appeared from behind my back to address the team. I think he was in awe of being in the presence of his heroes.

I told Samantha, the changing room went silent when Boulos walked forward and picked up the captain's football boots and began, what looked like, eating them.

She looked intrigued, as she tucked into her shakshuka. Here is what he had to say, and I didn't understand a word and probably neither will you.

تبدو لك حمولة من الرماة ، أنت مجموعة من الجنيات ، واجهت عديمة
الفائدة الحمار حفنة مثيرة للشفقة من الخاسرين ، كنت متعجرف ، وتعتقد أنك
جيد جدا ما يسمى لاعبي كرة القدم ، والاستماع لي ، يمكن أن تلعب قطتي كرة
القدم أفضل مما كنت الكثير ! أنت لا تستحق الأفضل ، ولا تستحقه ، ولم تكسبه
بأي شكل أو شكل أو شكل. أحذية كرة القدم هذه تنتمي إلى نجوم كرة القدم ،
الأفضل في العالم ، وليس لك. لقد كان أداؤك على مدار العامين الماضيين في
كأس آسيا بمثابة إهمال لبلدنا ، وإذا صادفنا أي فرصة للفوز بكأس العالم والتي
تبدأ في غضون شهرين فقط ، يتعين عليك إجراء معجزة.
لذا يبدأ التدريب غدًا ، ويبدأ فعلًا ولن ترتدي أحذية مثل هذه ، ستلعب على
قدمي الدب. نعم ، قدميك الدب حتى ينزف.
فكر في كلامي. تم طردك ، اذهب إلى منازلك وقد أمضيت ليلة مبكرة
ونحن ، القاضي وأنا ، سنراكم صباح الغد مبكرا ، نخرج من هنا ، نخرج !

So I've translated it for you via Google translate, so allow for the lack in coherence.

Look, you load of tossers, you bunch of fairies, you useless arse-faced pathetic bunch of losers, you arrogant, believe-you're-so-good so-called footballers, listen to me. My dogs could play better football than you lot! You do not deserve the best, you do not deserve to wear the Falcons colours, and you have not earned it in any way, shape or form. These football boots belong to soccer stars, the best in the world, not to you. Your performance over the last two years in the Asian cup has been a disgrace to our country and if we stand any chance of winning the World Cup, which starts in just two months' time, you, no, not you but I, have got to perform a miracle.

So tomorrow training starts, really starts and you won't be wearing boots like these, you will play in bare feet. Yes, your bare feet until they bleed.

Think on my words. You are dismissed, go to your homes, have an early night and we, the Judge and I, will see you tomorrow morning early, get out of here, get out!

203rd Day

Samantha and I are back at the manor, sitting on the sofa with Bogie in an armchair beside us and the dogs enjoying

Bonios at our feet and making a terrible mess. My cat, who had finally returned, snuggled up to Herbert and Rusty. They had both given up chasing her, respect had been earned, and they were now all the best of friends.

The TV was on and we were watching the World Cup final between England and Saudi Arabia taking place in Qatar.

There were eight minutes to go and the score, even after extra time, remained England 2-2 Saudi Arabia. There was to be a penalty shootout.

Bogie was screaming his heart out for England while Samantha and I cheered for our team. We were enjoying a special bottle of champagne I had fetched from the cellar, Bogie a lager, and the tension and the atmosphere was intense.

I couldn't believe it, but Boulos had done it; even if they lost the Saudis could be proud of themselves. I could not contain my excitement as the camera moved to showing Boulos striding up and down the touch line, his arms held high, screaming encouragement and direction to his team.

After Boulos' pep talk to the team in The King Fahd International Stadium, I made an easy decision and went to meet the Saudi Arabia Football Federation at their headquarters and told them I had put my personal chauffeur in charge of their team. I put my case in a judicial manner, which always worked, and I left the building pleased with the knowledge Boulos was now the new manager of the Falcons.

I'd returned to the Ritz Carlton, Samantha and I packed in a rush, and a new driver called Abdel Fattah drove us to the airport.

I used the short time before the penalty shootout to ask Bogie to fetch another bottle of champagne from the cellar, which he opened and then topped our glasses while he then retrieved another lager.

Now this is where history is made.

England won the toss and took the first shootout. It missed, hitting the bar.

It was the Saudis turn and it hit the back of the net.

England's go and the Saudis saved it.

Saudis turn and it hit the back of the net.

England; the ball went over the bar.
Saudis, and the England goalie managed to just touch the ball as it sped past into the net. The stadium, filled to capacity, erupted. Saudi Arabia had won the World Cup 3-0 on penalties!

Both Samantha and I were on our feet dancing around the coffee table while Bogie crushed his larger can and tossed it on the floor. I told him to pick it up immediately and put it in the bin. He disappeared to the kitchen with it and as he left he said he was going to bed.

Goodnight, we both said and then sat down, wanting to hear Boulos being interviewed. And there he was with his everlasting smile beaming at the world with celebrations including balloons and fireworks erupting around him.

"Congratulations Boulos, how may I ask, have you managed to achieve this amazing victory for your country?"

He looked quizzically at his interviewer and then replied, "I met an Englishman who gave me the chance."

Last Day

I feel I must leave it there. I have told you my story and however incredible you think it is, it is all true.

Samantha and I are going to live happily ever after, despite having to put up with Bogie, in my manor house with our adorable dogs.

To be fair to him, he has his uses, and has been a good friend, despite having murdered someone.

There was a special delivery today, all wrapped up in tissue and brown paper and surrounded in cardboard. Both Samantha and I ripped it open in front of the television and it now hung above the mantelpiece, replacing the copper hunting horn.

It was a painting of me, in tight blue swimming trunks, diving off a board into a swimming pool full of intensely blue water beside a modern house.

Attached to the back of the picture was an envelope and within, a plain card, which now rested on the mantelpiece below the painting.

Upon the card the following words were inscribed:

You've got to live life and make a splash! Well done, my friend, love David Hockney.

If you have liked my tale, I would like to reassure you, I am still recording my life in my little book. So until the next time, have a drink on me.

I recommend the Scotch.

Epilogue

You might think I have missed a lot of opportunities to create continuity during my recollections, but I have intentionally done this because I am a very important judge and I know much more than you!

You might think things have tended to happen sporadically and have been looking forward to seeing how the consequences turn out, but frequently there is nothing further.

You might find this a bit disappointing.

But don't worry.

As you know I've already got my pencil in hand to record, in my pocket diary, what happens next and perhaps more importantly, in more detail, what happened before!